Angel By My Side

LILY'S STORY

Other Avon Camelot Books in the
ANGEL BY MY SIDE *Trilogy by*
Erin Flanagan

AMELIA'S STORY

Coming Soon

GRACE'S STORY

Angel By My Side

LILY'S STORY

ERIN FLANAGAN

AN AVON CAMELOT BOOK

ANGEL BY MY SIDE: LILY'S STORY is an original publication of Avon Books. This work has never before appeared in book form.

AVON BOOKS
A division of
The Hearst Corporation
1350 Avenue of the Americas
New York, New York 10019

Copyright © 1995 by Erin Flanagan
Published by arrangement with the author
Library of Congress Catalog Card Number: 94-96888
ISBN: 0-380-78254-5
RL: 4.8

First Avon Camelot Printing: August 1995

CAMELOT TRADEMARK REG. U.S. PAT. OFF. AND IN OTHER COUNTRIES, MARCA REGISTRADA, HECHO EN U.S.A.

Printed in the U.S.A.

OPM   10   9   8   7   6   5   4   3   2   1

For David MacTavish

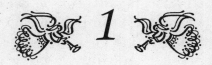

1

"**T**his is such a great way to end the summer! I love the Santa Monica beach and pier!" I shifted the beach umbrella to my other shoulder and followed Mom and my nine-year-old sister, Kate, over the hot sand.

I hummed along with the Beach Boys' song "California Girls" as it blasted out of somebody's radio.

"Did you guys know that Brian Wilson, the lead guy of the Beach Boys, went to high school right here in Southern California?"

"Oh, Amelia, everybody in California knows that," Kate said as she struggled to carry the drink cooler.

"Maybe, but did you also know that he *failed* his music class at Hawthorne High?"

"You're kidding?" said Mom. She stopped and

shaded her eyes, trying to find the perfect spot on the crowded beach.

"No, and not only that, the song he handed in that got him the *F* turned out later to be 'Surfin' Safari,' which was a big hit. Tons of people told him he would never make it in the music business because he was too young."

"Cyril says you should always carry an umbrella to use on all the people who will rain on your parade," Kate said firmly.

I shifted the umbrella again. "Then I guess I'm all set."

Kate turned to look at me, and as she did, the cooler slipped out of her hands, dropped in front of her, and she sprawled over it.

"Have a good trip? See you next fall!" I couldn't help laughing as I helped her up. "Hey, where's Cyril, your guardian angel, now? Shouldn't he catch you before you fall?"

"No." She brushed the sand off her tanned legs. "Sometimes you are supposed to fall."

"Oh." Her assurance made me pause. I took the cooler and handed her the umbrella. "Come on, hurry up. It looks as if Mom has finally found the perfect spot up ahead."

"Here you two, give me a hand with the blanket, will you?" Mom handed us each a corner of the old flowered quilt, and we laid it carefully on the sand. She anchored the corners with our junk.

"Okay, girls, you know the rules," Mom said as she slathered sun block on my back, and I slathered Kate's. "Nobody gets to bug me for one full hour. No questions, no cute-boy sightings, no food requests. Got it?"

"Okay, got it." I finished Kate and did Mom's back.

"But, Mom, what if I get really, really, really, super thirsty?" asked Kate.

"Then you should get a drink from the cooler," said Mom. She put on her sunglasses and staked the blue and white striped umbrella. The book she dragged out of her beach bag looked as if it weighed twenty-five pounds.

"Come on, Kate. Let's give Mom her break." I looked out at the glistening water and the blue bonnet skies. Good. No smog today. The pier jutted out clearly in the distance. "Want to go to the pier and ride the carousel?"

"Yeah! That's my favorite!" She churned away through the sand.

"Thanks," said Mom with a big smile.

"No problem." I ran to catch up with Kate. Running in sand feels just like when you run in a dream. Something unseen seems to hold you back.

"Wait up," I called.

"Hurry up!" she replied.

I caught up to her, grabbed her hand, and she started to skip. I tried not to. I'm not the type of thirteen-year-old girl who can look good and skip at the same time.

Maybe Wendy Lockwood, the prettiest girl in the school, if not on the whole planet, could do it. But not me.

I'm a trudger, I guess. Not a skipper.

"Aren't you so excited about junior high, Amelia?" Kate let go and danced ahead. "I'm excited for fourth grade. And the first day of school is only two weeks away."

"Don't remind me."

"I guess that means you're not excited."

"You guessed right." I waited while she executed two perfect cartwheels—something else I don't do. When she was right side up again, I continued: "I'll feel better when Shura comes back from her trip to Russia. I'm used to planning everything with her. I've really missed her this summer."

Kate stopped dead in her tracks. "Wait, Amelia."

"What for?"

"Cyril says to tell you that Shura is with you even when she's gone."

"What is that supposed to mean? I don't see her, so she's not with me."

Kate looked around, then pointed to a radio that someone turned on. "It's like that. You can't see radio waves, either. But there's music here."

"That's not the same thing."

"Is too."

"Is not." I shook my head and plowed on. This conversation, like many with Kate (and probably Cyril) was unnerving. I wanted to believe in guardian angels, but it was just too weird. And I had to remember, this was Southern California: land of fruits and nuts!

I paused when we reached the boardwalk and watched as the crowds moved in undulating waves. They reminded me of the colorful schools of fish pictured in our science book.

I closed my eyes and sniffed. Popcorn, cotton candy, corn dogs, and salty air mingled in my nostrils. *Ahhhh*. Summer.

Music from the calliope of the carousel conjured up images of circus animals.

Kate and I walked along the sandy boards and stopped at a tee-shirt shop. The artist inside was making original drawings on each shirt.

"Whatcha making?" asked Kate.

"Angels. They're really big right now." The guy paused, redid his ponytail, and smiled.

"They've always been big," replied Kate with her own knowing smile.

"Come on, let's go to the carousel; the line is getting long," I said.

"I love these horses," said Kate after we were in line. "Lots of stuff changes, but these always stay the same. Do you think they'll always be here, Amelia?"

"I hope so. They've been here ever since I can remember, and Mom said she came to the carousel when she was a little girl. That was eons ago."

Suddenly I wondered if time ran on and on, in a circle, just like these horses.

"My turn!" Kate jumped onto the carousel and ran from horse to horse, careful to choose the "right" one.

As the ride began I watched Kate go around and around on the beautiful, frozen-in-time creatures. I found myself thinking about guardian angels again. Did they go around and around through time? Could I possibly have one, too? Or were they really just imaginary friends?

I recalled the mysterious lady in white I had spoken to when I made a guest appearance on the "Candy K. Crowley" talk show. The lady had been in a corner of the greenroom, where guests have to wait. I had seen her again on a bus, and twice more over the summer. At least I thought I saw her.

She seemed to be watching me.

No. That wasn't quite it.

It was more like . . . waiting for me.

Could I have imagined her?

"Amelia, over here!" Kate called out as she rose up on her horse.

"I see you!" I waved. I gasped as Kate turned and started to slip off her horse. The safety belt dangled near her leg. I made a motion toward her, but she caught herself just in time.

Or did someone catch her?

We dragged our beach stuff and our hot, sandy selves up the walk to our apartment in the Tiki Village complex.

Kate stopped at her favorite Tiki and rubbed his brown, wooden tummy. She recited:

> *"Tiki, Tiki, standing tall,*
> *Grant my wishes,*
> *Grant them all."*

"What did you wish for?" Mom asked with a smile as she unlocked the door.

"Don't tell," I warned. "Then it won't come true."

"Yes, it will," said Kate as she raced past me to turn on the air conditioner.

"I thought there was a wish rule that if you tell, it won't work. Like on birthday candles." I went in the kitchen to empty the cooler. Kate followed, while Mom went to check the messages on the answering machine in her room.

"Wishes aren't secrets, Amelia," said Kate as she got down her favorite cup—the one with Winnie-the-Pooh on it—and filled it with grape juice.

"Okay, what did you wish, then?"

"I wished Mommy would marry Mr. C."

"Good wish. I wish that, too." I drank some of her juice. "In fact, I'd love it."

"Yep. He is so nice." She lowered her voice and asked, "Can blind guys be dads?"

"Sure they can." I took her thick hair and worked it into a braid. "Blind guys can do just about anything they want."

"You think he wants to?"

"Marry her?"

"Uh-huh."

"Seems like it. I mean, he's been hanging around all summer. And we all helped out at Bret Harte School with the summer program for the blind kids. I think he likes Mom a lot. And us, too."

"More than our real dad liked us before he left?" She turned to look up at me.

"Well, Mr. C. is still here, isn't he?"

"Yes." She turned away. "He sure is. He hasn't left us."

Mom came in just then and cleared her throat. "Who hasn't left us?"

"Mr. C. He likes us, and he hasn't left us. Right, Mommy?" Kate went over and wrapped herself around Mom.

"That's right, honey. He hasn't left. But even if he did, we'd be okay."

Something was up. Mom didn't sound like Regular Mom, she sounded like Worried Mom. And she was looking at me.

"Amelia, would you come into my room as soon as you've finished?"

"What's wrong?" I could see her eyes glisten in the harsh kitchen light. "What's happened?"

"Not here." She glanced down at Kate and shook her head.

"Why not here in front of me, Mommy? Is Amelia in trouble?" Kate planted herself at the kitchen table.

"It's not Amelia . . ." Mom finished the sentence with a silent shake of the head.

"Mommy's crying!" Kate's voice rose. "Amelia, Mommy's crying!"

We rushed to put our arms around our mother.

When your parents are divorced, and you live only with your mom, it is a very big deal if she cries. A BFD, as Shura always says.

"Was there a message on the machine?" I asked.

She nodded and blew her nose on a napkin. "Katie, get me a drink of water, would you, please? Then sit down here, okay?"

"Okay." Kate rinsed out her Winnie cup and filled it with water. She placed it before Mom as if it were a priceless, crystal goblet, which to Kate it was.

I wiped my palms on my shorts and waited anxiously.

Mom bit her lower lip and looked at Kate. "You girls are both old enough to hear this, I suppose." She sipped the water. "There was a message on the answering machine from Shura's grandparents, the ones who live with them, that I must call back right away. Which I did."

"Is Shura okay? Where is she?"

"She's . . ." Mom swallowed. "I am so sorry to tell you this, but they received word that there was a plane crash near Moscow. The plane that was carrying Shura and her parents. And, honey, there were no survivors. . . ."

"No!" I buried my face in my hands. "Oh, no!"

"Does it mean they're all dead?" whispered Kate.

"Yes," said Mom. "The grandparents are devastated. They only moved here to the U.S. to be close to Shura and her family. Now they're all alone."

I felt my mother's arms envelope me. Kate patted my hair. But the tears didn't come; they were caught somewhere. Somewhere in my heart, which hurt.

Mom cried for Shura and her family. Kate cried because Mom did.

I sat, stunned, and wondered how I would get along without my best friend.

Shura, the regal, confident swan who had sailed into my life when I was in kindergarten: I would be adrift without her.

My heart ached harder. Then a strangely familiar male voice whispered, "Death is a doorway, child, not a wall."

"Amelia, Cyril says death is a doorway . . ."

"Not a wall," we finished in unison.

I looked up. I had heard it, too.

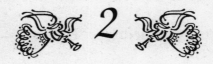

Shura's grandmother spoke broken English, and I strained to understand what she wanted.

"You would like me to call Shura's friends from school and ask them to come?" I moved the receiver to my other ear.

"*Dah*. To do this thing would be good. You will do?"

"Yes, I will. And the address you gave me a minute ago, is that for the synagogue?" I scribbled furiously on my notepad.

"*Dah*. And from synagogue to Beth Olam Cemetery."

"That's on Santa Monica Boulevard?"

"I think. Yes."

"Okay. I'll tell her friends. Many people will come."

"Spahseebah."

"You're welcome. Good-bye, Grandmother Na-jinsky."

"Dah sveedahneeyah, Amelia."

I hung up. *Dah sveedahneeyah*, Shur, I whispered.

Mom stuck her head in. "How are you doing?"

"Okay."

"Noel is here and we're about to eat dinner. You hungry?"

"Not really. I need to call some kids and tell them about Shura's funeral service."

"It's nice of you to help."

I nodded. "Tell Mr. C. I'll see him later, okay? I don't really want to talk to anybody right now."

"He understands. I'll save you some casserole." She dangled in the doorway. "Um. Amelia?"

"What, Mom?" I read over the list of names I'd been working on. I really wished she would leave me alone.

"There is a story called 'On Borrowed Time,' and it was made into a movie a long time ago. You might like me to rent it."

"I'm not in the mood for an old movie, Mom."

"Well, you might be for this one. It's about an old man who traps death up a tree and refuses to let him come down."

I looked up. "I wouldn't mind doing that myself right about now."

"I thought so. It's hard to understand when someone so young has to die."

"Why couldn't some really bad person die?" I swallowed and looked at her, waiting for an answer. But at some point I guess parents don't have any more answers.

"Anyway, thanks for offering the movie, Mom. Maybe we could watch it later. Like next week or next month or something."

"Sure." She closed the door.

I dialed Richard Flink's number. Richard and I had gone to the graduation dance together and had both volunteered over the summer at the blind school where Mr. C. is principal. I was in deep like with Richard.

"Hey," he said, "I heard the news. I can hardly believe it. Out of all the kids I know, Shura was the most alive of anyone. Like, bigger than life, or something."

"I know." I explained the funeral service stuff to him.

"My parents will want to come, too. Is that okay, do you think?"

"I'm sure it's fine. Listen, will you call some of the guys for me? It's kind of awkward. I mean, I'm still . . . I don't know"—I paused—"choked up about it."

"Sure. Let me get a pencil."

I heard him dump out half the stuff on his desk. "Go 'head."

After we split the list he said, "I know I'm always messing around and quoting Shakespeare, and driving you crazy . . ."

"Definitely."

"But he said some pretty cool stuff, and one thing he said about death was . . . do you want to hear it?"

"Yes."

"Good. He said, 'We are such stuff as dreams are made on, and our little life is rounded with a sleep.' "

I could hear Richard breathe. His adenoids gave him trouble.

"That is nice. I guess I'd rather just think of her as sleeping."

"You know, the Bard said some amazing stuff. Personally, I can't believe everybody thinks he's such a drag."

"Maybe most kids hate to read the plays because of the old language."

"Probably. Hey, I have a great book of his quotations, if you ever want to borrow it."

"Thanks, Richard. Maybe I will. I'm having trouble concentrating on regular books. I can't keep my mind off of Shura, and the plane, and wondering if she was scared . . . wondering what she thought just before . . ."

"I know. I know. So, let's go the zoo tomorrow."

"What?" I would never get used to Richard's sudden left turns in the middle of a conversation.

"We should go to the L.A. Zoo. It'll be good. Animals are so cool. They know how to hang out and just do nothing. That's what you should do."

"Maybe that would be good."

"Sure it would. We can take the bus. I'll come over tomorrow morning."

"If my mom needs to work at the hospital, I'll have to bring Kate."

"Bring the little Katerator. She always cracks me up."

"Thanks a lot, Richard . . . I . . ."

"Forget it. What are friends for? I'll bring my book of Bard quotes tomorrow, too. Might come in handy. See ya."

"See ya."

The next day was a perfect zoo day. Not too hot. Zoos don't smell too great on really hot days.

We rumbled over on the bus. Richard and Kate played I Spy.

"I spy . . . something brown!" said Kate.

Richard looked around. "I got it! The air!"

"No way, Flinkman." She looked out the window. "This is a low smog day. Guess again."

"*Ummmmm*. Amelia's hair."

"That's brown, but that's not it." Kate crossed her arms and waited.

If I were playing, I thought, I'd guess my life. My brown life had gotten even browner since Shura was gone. I stared out the window as we turned off the Golden State Freeway and onto Zoo Drive.

"I got it now, for sure!" crowed Richard. "It's my belt!"

"Nope. That's boring. You give up?"

"You got me. I give."

Kate smiled wickedly. "It was your little, teeny tiny whiskers that are trying to grow out of your chin!"

Richard rubbed his face thoughtfully. "Oh, of course, my beard. How did I ever miss that—it's as clear as the hair on my chin!"

"Yeah, all four of them," I teased.

"All right, all right. I will not have my manliness mocked!" He grinned and picked Kate up. "Off we go, Katerator, this is the zoo! Famous for its more than two thousand strange creatures!"

I followed behind them. "We'll fit right in," I said with a laugh.

We paid our admission and stood at the entrance, staring at the map.

"Now, the animals are grouped according to continent of origin." Richard squinted at the paper. "Shall we go to Africa, Eurasia, Australia . . . ?"

"Anywhere but the snake pit," said Kate.

"It's called the Reptile Pavilion," I corrected.

"That's just a nice name for the snake pit," she insisted.

I shrugged. "Okay, you guys decide. I don't care where we start. I just don't want to miss the swans."

As we strolled around the seventy-five-acre zoo, I realized Richard had been right. Something about the animals was calming. Maybe it was their dignity and playfulness, even in captivity.

Kate seemed to speak for all of us when she said, "If I could, I would let all these animals go back to their real homes. Even the snakes. I would set them all free."

"Me, too." Richard spotted the snack bar. "Hey, let's go get an ice cream."

"Okay!" Kate dug around in her Elvis Presley purse for her allowance. "You want one, Amelia?"

"No. You guys go ahead. I want to go over and watch the swans. Meet me there."

"Okay."

I walked over and leaned against the wooden railing of the swan pond. Suddenly a lady was next to me. I moved over to make room.

"They are lovely, don't you agree?" she asked.

I nodded. "I love them."

"Yes. Did you know people used to think that swans were mute?"

"No, I didn't."

"They thought that swans sang only one time—at the moment they died."

I turned abruptly toward her. "What did you say?"

She smiled and turned toward the pond. A swan came gliding over to her. "I said that it was believed that swans only sang at the moment of their death."

"Oh."

"Isn't that comforting?" She turned toward me, her blue eyes dancing.

"Yes, I guess it is." I gazed at her familiar face. She wore her blond hair high up off her neck. Her dress was white with little flowers embroidered at the edges. I furrowed my brow. Could this be the same lady I'd seen at the "Candy K. Crowley Show" last spring? I knew I had seen her before.

"I think the swans sang because they knew they didn't have to be afraid, don't you?" She smiled.

"Afraid of death, you mean?"

She nodded. "Certainly. After all, it's only a doorway. Isn't that so?"

My jaw dropped.

"Amelia!" called Kate.

I turned to the sound of my sister's voice. When I turned back, the lady was gone.

But not forgotten.

* * *

The funeral was long and sad and my dress was itchy. On top of all that, I was nervous. The Najinskys had asked me to say a word or two about Shura. I wrote some stuff down, but now it seemed so dumb. I crumpled the paper in my pocket.

Mom nudged me. "You're to speak next. You okay?"

"As okay as I'll ever be." I remembered how I had managed to get through the "Candy K. Crowley Show." I would do the same thing now. I cleared my throat, stepped up to the front, and wrapped my shaking hands around the microphone.

"Shura was my best friend since kindergarten, and she always reminded me of a swan. She was regal, and proud, like a swan." I swallowed and looked out at Richard. "A friend of mine gave me a book of quotes from Shakespeare, and I found something in there that is just for Shura." I closed my eyes and hoped my memory was working:

"' 'Tis strange that death should sing!
I am the cygnet to this pale faint swan,
Who chants a doleful hymn to [her] own death,
And from the organ-pipe of frailty sings
[Her] soul and body to their lasting rest.' "

I swallowed through my constricted throat and added, "You see, back then they thought that swans only sang as they died. And I think Shura is singing."

I sat down.

It was over.

Almost.

Two days later I went to visit Shura at Beth Olam Cemetery. I brought two gifts for her.

After I made sure no people were around, I talked out loud to my best friend.

"Listen, Shur. I can't come here a lot, and I know you understand. But I wanted to give you something." I removed my talisman from around my neck. It was the medal I had received from the kids at Bret Harte School for the Blind. "You were there when I won this, so you know what it means to me."

I read the inscription: "Wait for the day that maketh all things clear." I dug a deep hole and buried my gift.

Finally I cried. My hot tears made little circles in the dust. I shook my head and wiped the tears from under my glasses.

"Geez, Shur, I guess I'm still waiting for things to be clear."

I leaned back on my heels and looked around as I waited for my sobs to stop. It was sure quiet. And so still.

"Oh, yeah. One more thing." I unwrapped the

flowers I had brought and laid them down gently. "I brought you some lilies. They're flowers of peace, I think."

"What a lovely gesture."

The voice grabbed me, and would have knocked my socks off if I had been wearing any. I looked up into the eyes of the lady I'd seen at the zoo. The lady in white who had been watching, and waiting.

She touched a finger to my head. It tingled where she touched it.

"My name happens to be Lily," she said quietly. "And, Amelia, I am your guardian angel."

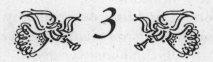 3

"*E*xcuse me. Young lady?"

"Yes, sir?" I turned to a new voice.

"I hate to disturb you, but we're about to close. There's another funeral later, and we have to get ready. You understand."

"Sure." I stood and brushed the dirt from my knees. The man seemed to believe I was alone. I looked around. I was.

I walked down the path and wondered if maybe the grief was getting to me. I had heard about people practically going crazy with grief. And here I was, in a graveyard, having visions of angels! It was okay for a little kid to believe in this guardian angel stuff, but I was not a little kid. Just a very sad big one.

The Tiki grinned crazily at me as I headed up

the walk to our door. I stopped and stared at him. "I wish," I whispered, "that I really did have an angel."

I felt a presence behind me, to the left. I turned quickly. Nothing there.

"Mom! Kate!" I called as I went in the apartment. No answer. I smiled and tried two more entities. "Cyril! Lily!" No answer again.

There was a note, though. It read: "Dear Amelia, I took Katie school shopping. The big day is tomorrow! We'll be home by dinner time. Love, Mom."

Argh. School. I decided to take a nap, rather than face my thoughts and fears.

The phone jangled me out of my peaceful dreams.

"Ah, hullo?" I tried to sound awake.

"Were you sleeping?" It was Richard.

"Sort of."

"Enjoying 'the honey-heavy dew of slumber?' "

"Sort of." I yawned. "What did you say?"

"Not me. Julius Caesar said it. Act two, scene one."

"Oh. What's up?"

"My mother, for one thing. She insists we go shopping and get the dreaded school supplies. Since they're shoving me into private school this year, I need better junk and more of it. You want to go with us?"

"Yeah. I probably should. Mom and Kate already went. Can you give me about half an hour to wake up and stuff?"

"Sure. 'And stuff' can take forever. I hate that."

"Ha ha. Thanks for asking me to come along, Richard."

"My mother made me."

"Oh, *Richard*."

"I'm kidding. You're welcome. See you at four. Bye."

"Bye."

At four on the dot I climbed into the backseat of the Flink family station wagon.

"Hi, Mrs. Flink." Richard's mom had short, graying hair, and she always wore a jumper and flat shoes. She looked trustworthy, like an old girl scout.

"Good afternoon, Amelia. I'm so happy you were able to join us. The mad march of September begins again!"

I loved talking to Richard's English professor parents. I figured it was good for my vocabulary.

"I meant to tell you, dear, how moved I was by the words you offered at the service last week. It was simply lovely." She glanced at me in her rearview mirror.

"Thank you."

"You are most welcome."

Richard launched into a description of all the

25

things he refused to wear to school this year. I was grateful for the change of subject.

"I hope you don't mind, Amelia," said Mrs. Flink, "but we must stop briefly at Richard's orthodontist."

"I don't mind," I said.

"I lost my rubber bands." Richard lifted his top lip. "See? Right over here is where I hafta hook it—"

"Richard! Take your hands out of your mouth! I'm sure Amelia does not want to be given a tour of that miasmic landscape!"

He grinned. "Sorry."

"It's okay." I smiled.

The thought of kissing Richard had crossed my mind once or twice, but between his braces, my glasses, and our awkwardness, I knew it wouldn't happen. At least for a while. And that was okay with me.

Richard scratched his nose. Where did people put their noses when they kissed anyway?

I had watched kissing scenes carefully in the movies, but none of the actors had braces, glasses, or acne. Something told me it wouldn't be as smooth in real life.

"Excuse me?" I leaned toward the front seat as Mrs. Flink's question brought me back to the station wagon.

"I was just saying, dear, I wonder if you're all

ready for junior high school?" She pulled the wagon into a parking space, and Richard ran into his orthodontist's office.

"I guess I'm ready. I am a little nervous, though. The junior high is a lot bigger, and we have to change classes and remember two different locker combinations. But I'm sure I can do it." I wasn't sure of any such thing, but parents expect to hear it.

"I'm sure you'll do fine. After all," she turned and smiled at me, "you have been on national television. You handled yourself very well."

"Thank you." I knew she would never believe that junior high was even more frightening than TV. After all, the television show was over in an hour, and all I had to do was answer some questions about why I didn't feel pretty. Junior high would take three years, and I still wasn't going to be pretty!

I felt a tingle on my forehead. It made me shiver.

"Let's hit the road, Mom!" said Richard as he clambered back into the car. "Floor it!"

"In a station wagon, Richard?" she asked with a laugh.

"You've got to make the best of what you've got, Mom! That's what Dad always says!"

We floored it, at forty-five miles per hour, all the way to the mall.

* * *

27

Hollywood Junior High was huge. I stood in front of the entrance clutching my schedule. A zillion people hurried around me.

My breath was coming in short gasps, so I made myself relax and take a deep breath. I could almost hear Shura say, "Come on, this is no BFD. It's just a school. And, basically, they're all the same—prisons with bad food."

That's true, I thought. I shifted my pack and headed up the steps. Just inside the door there was a table with two older kids, a girl and a boy, giving directions.

"Could you tell me where locker 237 is? And then where would I find this math class?" I handed over my sweaty schedule.

The boy, who was as cute as they come, which made me as nervous as they come, looked at my schedule. "Okay, go down this hall and up the stairs," he pointed and looked at me. "See?"

"Uh-huh. Then?"

"Then your locker will be on the left side, 'cause it's an uneven number. And your class is at the end of that hall. Okay?" He grinned and gave me back the sheet of paper along with a map of the school. His eyes were *so* blue.

Still looking at him, I took the paper. Maybe that's why I didn't see the box of school maps that I tripped over as I turned to go.

Laughter rang out around me and echoed down

the halls. The cute guy helped me up. He had to lift me and keep a straight face all at the same time. I don't know how he did it.

The girl at the table looked superior and disgusted, all at the same time. I don't know how she did it.

There wasn't time to cry, so I brushed myself off, thanked him without making eye contact, and hurried to my first class.

Junior high was already a disaster. And I'd only been there five minutes!

As I slid into a back chair in my math class, I looked out the window and saw Lily. She hovered outside under a eucalyptus tree. She pressed her hands against the window pane, then disappeared. The words "I am here" hung in my mind.

Was I seeing her because I wanted her to be there—kind of like I used to think I saw my dad after he first moved out?

Even if she's a figment of my imagination, I decided she is a comfort. Especially since Shura's gone, and Richard's parents decided to send him to private school.

School was going to be a game of solitaire this year, I thought.

At lunch time, I searched for a friendly face from grade school. It was like looking for a gold stud earring on a patterned kitchen floor. I'd have to step on somebody to find one!

I settled at the edge of a table in the corner near the front. There was a sudden commotion at the door.

"Now, I can't eat with both of you guys, come on! There is only one of me, after all!" Wendy Lockwood smiled and gazed at her admirers. It looked as if junior high was not going to be a problem for her. Of course.

She wore a plaid miniskirt, a white blouse, and one of those cute, short, fuzzy black sweaters. The ribbon in her bouncy blond hair was plaid.

Somehow she knew what was popular to wear, even before it was popular!

"Oh, hey there, Amelia!" She headed toward me with a bright smile and a happy wave.

"Hi, Wendy," I said, hurriedly swallowing my bologna on white bread.

"I've hardly seen you at all this summer. Where have you been?" She slid gracefully into the awkward attached-to-the-table bench. Her fans followed suit.

"Oh, I've been around. Home, the beach, you know." I drank some milk.

"*Mmm-hmmm.*" She gestured at the boys around her. "Did you guys know Amelia was on the 'Candy K. Crowley Show' last June?"

They tore their eyes off her. You could almost hear a velcro-like *RIIIIIIP*.

"Oh, yeah?" said admirer number one. "How come you got to be on?"

"Well, it was no big deal, really." I shoved my trash into my lunch sack.

"Sure it was a big deal." Wendy genuinely thought she was helping me. "The whole show was about Amelia and how she didn't feel pretty, and how hard it is and everything."

The guys snickered.

"Let me get this straight," said admirer number two, "you got to go on a TV talk show because you're ugly?"

"Like, you're famous for it?" asked number one.

"No! Not like that," said Wendy. "It was different than that, right Amelia? I'm just terrible at explaining things!"

I didn't need a mirror to know my face was crimson. "That's right, it was different," I said, packing up my stuff. "I've really got to go, Wendy. I'll see you around, I guess."

"Oh, okay." She wiggled her fingers at me. "Geez, I almost forgot, I'm real sorry about Shura. I know you were best friends for practically your whole lives. That was so terrible. You know, how it happened and everything."

I nodded and hurried away.

After dinner that night I sat at the kitchen table making book covers out of paper sacks and contemplating the three years of agony that seemed to be glaring at me, like a gargoyle from the future.

Mr. C. came in and sat down. "What have we here?"

"The annual covering of the books," I replied.

"May I help you?"

"Sure." I was never surprised at all the things he could do. I had learned to follow his lead.

"Okay, good. I'm happy to be of service. You cut the appropriate size from the bag, and I'll do the folding."

"Where is my mom?" I measured the paper and my words carefully. I did not want him to know what a lousy day I'd had. He could pick up entire moods from a single word.

"She's reading to Katie. I think they're digging into *The Time Machine* by H. G. Wells."

I watched as his gentle hands deftly folded the paper. "Yes, Kate is on a sci-fi kick this week." I wrote my name across the paper-covered book.

"I have a favorite story by Wells," he said.

"Really? Which?"

"It's called 'The Country of the Blind.' "

"I never heard of it." I put the scissors down.

"It's not one of the better known." He kept folding. "It's about the adventures of a sighted person who accidentally comes upon a valley whose inhabitants are all blind."

"That sounds interesting," I said. "I would really like to read it."

"I have it. I could bring it sometime if you like. My father used to read it to me. Perhaps you could read it aloud."

I flushed, pleased. "I'd like that."

"And I'd like you to. Good practice for aspiring actresses." He smiled and continued: "My favorite part of the story is about how the blind people, hidden in this valley, think the air around them is alive with singing angels."

"Angels?"

He did not stop folding. "Yes. See, they can hear very well, of course, being blind, and they assume that what they hear flapping and singing just beyond their reach are bands of angels."

"Oh, but it's really birds, right?"

"That's another possibility," he said quietly. "But I kind of like the other idea, don't you?"

"Yes, I do. It would be nice if the air was filled with singing angels instead of"—my voice caught—"other stuff."

"The first day of school is always the roughest," he said. "But it gets better."

He had caught me again. I sighed. "I hope so."

"You know, time heals all wounds. But in the case of junior high, it is time wounds all heels." He smiled over his folding.

I laughed. "That would be good, too."

* * *

That night I woke from a sound sleep to see Lily sitting on the edge of my bed.

"I'm dreaming you, aren't I?"

"No, you're not," she replied, smoothing the delicate material of her dress.

"Why are you here now?" I asked.

"I've always been here."

"But why can I see you—"

"*Shhhh*." She smiled and touched her finger to my forehead. It tingled. "Feel that?"

"Yes."

"Have you always felt it?"

"Yes."

"Well, it's always been me. Unseen, but nearby."

I stared at her, my eyes filling with tears. "Thank you."

"Don't cry," she whispered. "I'm going to show you how to have a light blue life."

She touched my eyelids, and I fell asleep.

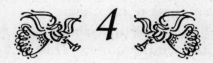

*W*hy did we have to play baseball with the boys?

Who decided organized exercise was healthy?

Whose big idea was it to make us take showers during school, anyway?

These were the questions that careened through my mind as Miss Timmerman, our gym teacher, explained the rules for her class.

"I liked P.E. better in grade school," whispered the girl sitting next to me. She was small and stick-skinny with blond, frizzy hair. Earlier I had heard somebody call her Q-Tip.

"I could deal with dodge ball, jump rope, and tether ball," continued Q-Tip. "But I draw the line at showers."

"Me, too," I whispered.

"Public group nudity should be against some school law, or something," she said.

"You ladies want to come up here to the front and share your fascinating conversation with the rest of us?" demanded Miss Timmerman.

"No," we squeaked in unison.

"Fine. Then listen up." She waved what looked like a white handkerchief. "This is your shower towel; only one to a customer, please. You will pick it up at the shower door and deposit it in the laundry bags on your way out. And the towels better be wet, because you better get wet!"

"I don't see any towel," said a girl in the back, "it looks more like a baby wipe!"

"I hear that every year," said Miss Timmerman with a roll of the eyes. "It's plenty big enough. We're all girls here. You don't need a beach towel, for heaven's sake. In the spirit of good hygiene, you will shower each and every day, and you are not excused if you have your period. Don't bother pleading with me."

A community moan rose. Everybody started whispering. We sounded like the angry villagers in the crowd scene of an old horror movie, anxious to let Dr. Frankenstein have a piece of our minds. Not to mention our torches.

"This is easy for her to say," whispered Q-Tip. "*She* doesn't have to shower. And she's probably too old to have her period."

"Probably." I smiled. "Hey, um, my name is Amelia Fleeman."

"Hi. Luana Gleeson. My enemies call me Q-Tip. My friends call me Lu."

"Hi, Lu."

"Okay, settle down," crowed Miss T. "Everybody turn around and face your locker. Try to get it open, then get undressed for your first shower. I'll time you today so you can get a feel for how long it'll take." She blew her whistle. *"Go!"*

Arms flew, bras snapped, and thirty girls jumped.

"Oh, no!" I struggled with my P.E. tee shirt, which wouldn't come off. "Luana, help me, I'm stuck."

She hopped over, one leg out of and one leg into her shorts. "Oh, it's your bra; it's snagged on the hem." She freed me and hopped back to her locker.

"Thanks!" I called as I tore off the rest of my clothes.

I couldn't help but notice some of the girls around me. Boy, there sure was a wide range of development in junior high!

"Let's go, let's go, let's go!" yelled Miss Timmerman. "Hit those showers, but no running!"

Lockers slammed and echoed. We trotted, a naked stampeding herd to the pit of horrors beyond. Lots of us were blushing—big time.

I shot into the pink and white tiled shower and tried to avoid anyone's eyes.

The water was icy cold and we squealed like seals.

"Just get damp!" yelled Lu over the screams and the cascading water.

I nodded and dipped in and out of the stream as quickly as possible. I didn't even bother with the soap dispenser.

At the sound of the whistle, we headed for the towels, arms crossed protectively in front.

Lu and I grabbed our towels and darted to our lockers. We dried fast and got dressed faster.

"I cannot believe this," moaned Luana as she yanked her socks on. "We have this to look forward to every single day."

"Oh, brother!" I groaned as my jeans got stuck when I tried to drag them up my still-wet legs. "This is completely and totally insane!"

"Welcome to junior high," said Luana.

That afternoon on the bus ride home I thought of Shura, and how I wished she was sharing the agonies of junior high with me.

My memories of her haunted the familiar streets of Hollywood. I looked out the window as Mann's Chinese Theatre passed by. Shura and I had fit our feet into the cement footprints there last year.

There was the Hollywood Wax Museum where we had posed with waxy stars.

And there was Shura's favorite place: the purple and pink tower of Frederick's of Hollywood, where they sold weird, sexy underwear.

Shura loved to go inside and stare at the Celebrity Lingerie Hall of Fame. Madonna's bra lived there until somebody stole it. Shura always said she hoped somebody was using it to feed their cats! No wonder we called it Frederick's of Hollyweird.

"Shura would have known how to handle junior high," I said quietly and sadly to the passing scenery.

"Yes, she would have." Lily was suddenly next to me. I could see her clearly. "But you know how to handle it, too," she added.

"I don't really believe that!" I said, staring at her.

"You didn't used to believe in me, either, did you?" She smiled and put her head to one side. "Well?"

"No-o-o," I admitted.

"So just because you didn't believe in something, didn't mean it wasn't there all along, waiting patiently to be discovered, did it?"

"I guess so." I thought for a minute. "Is it like how people didn't used to believe in black holes in space, and the holes were just sitting out there all that time?"

"Yes, like that. Black holes were there, whether you believed in them or not. The discoverer uncovers that which already is, Amelia."

"And you were there, too, no matter what I believed, right?"

"Yes." She smiled and folded her hands.

"You came because I needed you."

"I came because you were seeking something."

"Will you stay forever?"

"Yes. But I'll fade from your sight and from your memory when the time is right."

"I hope the time is never right." Now that I had Lily in my sights, I didn't want to let her go. I had a sudden urge to hug her, but I had a feeling she couldn't be grasped, only sensed.

"The time will come for parting; it always does," she said serenely. "But not today. Today we will ride the bus and think of Shura. And maybe you'll tell me about some of the girls you've met at junior high school."

"Okay," I said. "I'd like that."

Our bus stopped and two old ladies shuffled down the aisle toward the back exit. One of them pointed her cane at me and said to her friend, "Stay away from that loony little gal back there, she's been talkin' to herself ever since she got on this old bus!"

"I'm just talking to my guardian angel," I said with a wave and a smile.

The old lady stopped, readjusted her K-Mart shopping bag, and jabbed the air with her cane. "Oh, well, that's different. We could use us some more kids talking to angels. Lord knows we could!"

"You got that right!" agreed the second old lady as she clambered down the steps. "I'm all for that. Los Angeles was named after the angels, and I wish more of them would be flying around here, instead of bullets."

The doors closed behind them with a *whoosh*.

"We angels have quite a good reputation, as you can see," said Lily with a smile. "And we don't even run commercials on the television!"

"Speaking of television, were you there when I went on the 'Candy K. Crowley Show'?"

"Yes."

"You were in the greenroom, right?"

"That's right. I was the lady in white. As usual." She waved the gauzy white material of her dress.

"I thought so."

Lily smiled and raised her eyebrows. "You knew so."

"Okay, maybe I knew so, but I didn't want to. Not right then."

"You weren't ready until you heard about Shura. Just as Katie was not ready until your father left your family. Then she saw Cyril."

"Wow! Do you know Cyril?"

Her laugh was like the tinkle of tiny silver bells. "Of course I know Cyril."

"So, does everybody have an angel, Lily? Mom, Mr. C., everybody?"

"Certainly."

"Why can't everybody see or feel their angel?"

"You have to seek in order to see. Not many people seek. I'm not sure why."

"I think they're too busy shopping," I said matter-of-factly.

"Perhaps you're right. They're shopping for happiness, the poor dear souls."

"Happiness is slippery," I said. "After I was on the 'Candy K. Crowley Show,' I thought I would be happy forever."

"And?"

"And I found out that just because I talked about feeling like an ugly duckling, didn't mean I wasn't one anymore." I sighed and put on a smile I didn't feel.

"I wonder," she tapped her full lips with her fingertips, "do you think some of the girls you met at school today feel the same way?"

"Like ugly ducklings? Sure."

"Hmmmm. How sad. People are so caught up with packages."

I sat up straighter. "Well, yes, Lily, that's easy for you to say! Look at your package! Why, you're beautiful! I'll bet you were always beautiful!"

"I like that about you, Amelia. You speak your mind when you are truly moved!" She laughed at my surprised look and continued: "I take on a physical presence only to be seen by you. And if it is pleasing, it is because you see me with loving eyes." She touched my forehead. The familiar tingle circled my head.

Along with it came an idea.

"I wish I could help other girls who feel like me," I said suddenly. "Like, today at school, I met these girls who were called ugly names. I know how rotten that feels."

"And I suppose there are many other girls who feel this way as well?"

"Oh, I'm sure of it," I responded. "There are hordes of us. A bunch of ugly ducklings, paddling around the pond, looking for shelter."

"It must be, then, that you've all forgotten the most important point of the tale penned by Hans Christian Andersen."

"What do you mean?"

"Don't you remember, Amelia? The ugly duckling was really a swan—he just didn't believe it."

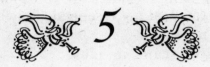

5

"**I**'m sorry I'm late, I got the tail of my shirt caught in my locker. It, ah, jammed, and the janitor had to get me out." My tardy excuse sounded even dumber when I had to say it in front of the whole class.

The snickering didn't help.

"Now, now, now, class, quiet down. These things happen in the seventh grade, they just do," clucked Mrs. Clark, the sewing teacher. She was short, fat, and feathery, reminding me of a hen.

Her sewing paraphernalia served double-duty as her jewelry: a wrist pincushion for a bracelet; a dangling tape measure as a necklace. Scissors hung in a holder from her belt, like a sword of sewing.

"Now that we are all here, I want you to get into

44

groups of two or three and gather around a sewing machine. We will learn how they work today, and even use them a little bit! Won't that be exciting!" Mrs. Clark waited for an enthusiastic response that never came. "You'll all come around after you've made your very own gym bag. I'm sure of that!"

More silence.

I glanced around my table. I hated getting into groups, especially at the beginning of a new school year. I was always afraid I'd be the one extra "leftover" kid, who would have to pair up with the teacher.

Girls were quickly getting into groups and grabbing all the newer sewing machines. I approached a machine with two pretty girls standing next to it. "Hi. You guys mind if—"

"Sorry," said one of the girls, "Amber is with us; she's just getting her stuff."

I blushed. "Oh, okay." I moved out of the way of a pretty red-haired girl who joined them.

They smiled and closed ranks.

"I'm alone," said a voice. I turned to see a tall, thin girl with thick glasses leaning on an ancient black Singer.

"Thanks," I said, approaching her. "This is almost as bad as choosing sides for basketball in P.E."

She laughed. "I know what you mean." She

pushed the heavy glasses up. "I'm Carol Duffy."

"Hi, Carol. I'm Amelia—"

"Quiet, please!" said Mrs. Clark, who stood on a stool at the front of the room. "Now let us get to know our machines, ladies, and remember, safety first!"

We were talked through the wondrous workings of our sewing machines.

"Have you ever done any sewing?" whispered Carol.

"No. My mom doesn't have time to sew, and we don't have a sewing machine. The most I've done is get a button back on. Barely."

"Yeah, if my hem falls, I pin it up."

"Did you get the stuff the teacher said about the bobbin?" I asked.

"No. I got lost on threading the needle!"

"Don't worry, we'll figure it out."

Mrs. Clark clapped her hands. "Ladies, we will begin with the threading of our machines; each group choose someone to go first. I will come around and check on your progress."

"You want me to go?" I asked.

"No," Carol said wearily. "I better do it. Otherwise I'll put it off forever." She hunched over the machine and popped a spool of thread on the holder. "So far, so good," she said.

"Run it through that little thingy," I said, pointing.

Between the two of us, Carol got it threaded successfully. My turn went smoothly, too.

The bell rang and Carol accidentally shoved her chair back into the aisle and onto the foot of Amber.

"Great! Right on my brand new white shoes, you four-eyed freak!" Amber shoved the chair back, nearly dumping Carol to the floor in the process.

"I'm sorry," said Carol.

"People like you always are," retorted Amber, "and with good reason!"

I'd been on the receiving end of remarks like that all my life. But still I stood by as Amber and her friends taunted Carol. If I tried to help, they'd start in on me.

A tingle passed down my spine.

I couldn't see Lily, but I knew she was there, and I knew why.

"Leave her alone," I said. "She said she was sorry. And it was an accident, anyway." I swallowed what felt like a hair ball in the back of my throat.

"Just shut up, ugly," said one of Amber's pretty friends. "Nobody was talking to you. Go get caught in your locker."

They laughed and walked away.

Carol went back to the table and got her backpack. I smiled at her, wanting her to be okay. "Oh well, creeps will be creeps," I said. She didn't reply.

"Listen, are you okay? 'Cause I don't want to be late for English, so I really ought to go now."

She looked at me through the thick lenses. "I've got to go, too. I've got to go redraw myself."

"What do you mean?"

"I'm like an Etch-A-Sketch drawing. I work so hard to look just right and be just right every day, but somebody always comes along and shakes me up."

I watched her walk away. Then I remembered. If you shake an Etch-A-Sketch, the picture disappears.

"I'll see you tomorrow!" I called out to her. But she was gone.

English class was in another building, and I ran to get there before the bell rang. I slid into my seat just in time.

"Settle down, everybody," said Mr. Jacobs, the teacher. "I have a reading assignment for you, and due to budget cuts, you will all have to find your own copy of the book we'll be reading." He held up a copy of *The Diary of Anne Frank*, and continued, "I'm sure you'll have no trouble finding one. It's a classic. Libraries and bookstores always have it in stock."

Our apartment has it in stock, too, I thought. I didn't mind reading the book again; it was one of my favorites. I'd always been intrigued with the idea of a young girl who wrote her own story, in her own words.

At the thought, a tingle ran around my head and down my back. I sat up.

What if somebody could write a book that told the story of all the ugly duckling girls, just as Anne Frank had told her story?

And what if that somebody was me?

I dismissed the thought. How silly. I laughed to myself. Who would listen to me? Impossible!

But the thought wouldn't leave me in peace. It followed me around all day, like a bad mood.

It even followed me home, where it got side-tracked by my sister.

"Hi, Kate," I said as I walked in the door and dumped my stuff on the couch. She was watching television. I clicked it off.

"Hey! I get to watch until you come home, Mom said."

"Well?" I held my hands out. "Here I am."

"That's no fair. It's 'The Brady Bunch' where Jan gets glasses and she feels all ugly, so she doesn't wear them, and she crashes her bike. It's my favorite."

"You know all 'The Brady Bunch' episodes by heart," I said firmly. "Why don't you start your homework?"

"No way, José. I don't want to." She flipped over

on her back and started to kick the edge of the couch. "That's boring."

"Stop kicking the furniture."

"Make me."

I thought quickly. I felt like poking her, but knew I couldn't. How did Mom handle Kate when she got cranky? Oh, yeah, distract her!

"I don't want to make you; I have to make dinner." I saw Kate smile, so I continued, "And you could help if you want."

She jumped up and charged into the kitchen. "Okay! Cooking is so fun!"

I shook my head and followed. She'd be sick of cooking as soon as she *had* to do it all the time.

"Can I decide what we're going to have?" she asked, scanning the pantry shelves.

"Sure. Decide away." I got a diet drink from the fridge and watched her. "So how's school so far?"

"Okay." She got out two boxes of macaroni and cheese. "I like my teacher, Miss Meredith. She is so-o-o-o pretty. And I like this one girl in my class named Beth, and we're almost best friends."

"And how's Cyril? Does he like it?"

"Oh, he's okay, I guess." She got four oranges out and rolled them on the counter. "Mr. C. is coming for dinner again, so I need all these oranges. And after dinner, he promised to play cards with me. He has a special deck of cards."

"Cyril promised to play cards?"

She gave me a stern look. "No, silly, Mr. C. promised."

I nodded. "I see."

"So we have the macaroni and the oranges, what else do we need?" She stood with her hands on where her hips would be if she had any.

"We need a veggie."

"Okay, *ummmm*," she thought, "how about carrots?"

"This dinner is going to be kind of orange, isn't it?"

"So? It's my favorite color." She burrowed into the vegetable cooler. "And it's Mr. C.'s favorite color, too."

"How could he have—"

"Remember, he could see when he was a little boy? Then he got blind. But he remembers orange. He told me."

"That's right, I forgot. He lost his sight when he was four or five."

"So, anyway, I want to give him orange food." She dumped the carrots onto the counter and blew a wisp of hair from her eyes. "I think he'll know it's orange. It is not impossible. I think he'll taste it and know. Do you think orange has a taste?"

I pulled gently on her ponytail. "I think you're a neat kid."

She smiled. "Me, too," she said as she happily counted out four carrots.

I cleared the kitchen table and set my homework out. That way I could keep an eye on the cook while I started my assignments.

As I watched the orange dinner take shape, I recalled my own wish for a light blue life, and Lily's willingness to help me get it. But how?

"You know," said Kate as she peeled a carrot, "orange really is my most favorite color, but it will be even favoriter if I can give it to Mr. C."

Suddenly a childhood rhyme fell into my brain:

The love in your heart wasn't put there to stay,
Love isn't love till you give it away.

"That's *it!* This is all connected!" I yelled, slamming my hand down on my math book.

"You scared me! I almost peeled me instead of the carrot! What's *it*?"

"The way for me to have a light blue life is to try to give something good away!"

"That sounds nice," said Kate.

"Indeed it does," said Lily, who appeared behind me.

I watched Kate. She didn't react to Lily.

"She can't see me," said Lily. "It's fading for her. She found what she was seeking."

"In Mr. C.?" I asked.

Lily nodded, floated over, and waved a hand over Kate's head. Another angel appeared. I knew it was Cyril. I realized I had seen him before, I just didn't know it at the time. He doffed his hat and bowed, then faded away.

"What did you say about Mr. C.?" asked Kate.

"Nothing. Just that I'm glad he's coming here."

"Yeah. Me, too." Kate grinned. "Will you make some orange juice to drink, Melia? I know that will be just the right thing."

"Sure." I got the frozen concentrate out. "I know just the right thing now, too."

My little sister hadn't sidetracked me after all.

6

"The idea to write a book about ugly ducklings came easily enough, but how am I supposed to actually do this?" Two days after coming up with my brilliant idea, I was at a brilliant-idea impasse. I flopped on my bed and stared at the ceiling. "Nobody is going to listen to me, I'm too young."

"That's what they said to Brian Wilson, too. Ever heard of the Beach Boys?" Lily made her point and continued, "Besides, I'm listening to you." She sat on Kate's bed and stroked the stuffed animals.

"Ye-e-e-es, but you have to listen to me. Don't you?"

"No. I want to." She drew her legs up and placed her chin on her knees. "If you want something enough, you have to *see* it first."

"I'm trying. But it's dark, and it's hard to see in the dark." I threw my little decorator pillows in the air and caught them. "Here I am, a thirteen-year-old kid with no writing experience, and I don't even know what to do first."

"Amelia, if you don't believe in me, you won't see me. And if you don't believe in your book, you won't see that, either."

I sighed. "Why don't you just make the book happen with angel magic? Can't you throw angel dust in people's eyes or flutter your wings around, or something?"

She laughed and shook her head. "No way, José, as your sister says. That is not how this works. If I do it, you won't learn from it. I'm not here to do for you what you can do for yourself." She pushed her sleeves up with determination. "Although I could if I wanted to, say, in an emergency. Angels may physically intervene during times of great peril or great evil. This is neither."

"I know. I just thought I'd try."

"Remember, Anne Frank was young and she wrote a book that could be published. And not long ago a little girl who lived through the war in Bosnia had her diary published, too."

"That's true. I heard about it at school." I held the little pillow to my chest. "And, to me, this is just as important." I sat up. "I mean, I really do believe in this idea. It's awful how so many girls feel so ugly. We're in some kind of a war zone, too, in our own way."

"Good thinking. So what's next? Try to think of one thing at a time, then it's not so overwhelming."

"First, I guess I need to talk to some of the girls so I can understand how they feel about being ugly ducklings—"

"*Think* they are ugly ducklings," corrected my angelic coach.

"Right. Think we are. Believe we are." I went over to the mirror and studied my reflection. My fine brown hair was stuck behind my ears. My glasses covered up my best feature, my dark brown eyes. My chin was kind of broken out. "I believe I would like to collect, in a book, stories from these girls about their lives—in their own words—and then I'd like to call it *Swan Songs*," I said quietly.

Lily appeared behind me in the mirror. "That is a fine idea and a beautiful title, dear Amelia, and no truer words could be spoken. Swan songs they are indeed." She touched the top of my head, and when I looked at my reflection, I hadn't changed on the outside; but something was shining through my eyes that had not been there before.

"Hey, Amelia, Mom wants to know if you want to come out and watch the 'Miss America Pageant' with us." Kate came up behind me and Lily hovered nearby.

"No, thanks. Not this year. I have something more important to do. It's a BFD."

"Okay. But we're having popcorn and grape soda in wine glasses." She waited to see if the lure would work.

"Save me some." I watched her ponytail bob out of the room, then I started to work on an outline for my book. Boy! What a sound . . . My Book.

An hour and a half later I closed my notebook and the phone rang.

"Hello?"

"Hi, Amelia, it's me, Richard the First."

"Hi! How's life in private school?"

"I'm surrounded by rich knaves and scurvy fellows. So, in other words, it's just like public school, only it costs more."

"I thought it was supposed to be a whole lot harder."

"Nah, that's a nasty rumor started by the private school officials to make parents think they're getting more bang for their educational buck. How's regular school?"

"Pretty regular. Only now we seventh graders are the lowliest worms."

"Ah, even the smallest worm will turn, being trodden on!"

"Shakespeare got that right!" I said, laughing.

"He usually does. So, who do you eat lunch with now?"

"Nobody in particular. I got caught at Wendy Lockwood's table once, but I didn't fit in with her crowd. I ate alone a couple times, but I've met a few new girls, and one of them asked me to eat with her today."

"Good. I was worried about you, what with Shura being gone and all."

"Thanks for worrying, but I'm okay. I miss her mostly during school and on weekends. It's hard not having a best friend around when you're so used to it. It's not so bad after dinner, because at night I can keep busy."

"Speaking of keeping busy, you want to go to the Griffith Park Observatory tomorrow night? My parents are going, too, but they won't sit with us or anything."

"I'd love to! Did you know they filmed *Rebel Without a Cause* up there? We'll be walking where James Dean actually walked!"

"Yeah, only you'll be accompanied by the rebel with a clause: c-l-a-u-s-e. Get it?"

"Har, har. I get it. I got it. It's good."

"Thank you. Hold your applause until I see you on the morrow."

"What time?"

"Ah, time, the inaudible and noiseless foot of time—"

"You better make it audible."

"Okay. I think my mom said we'd leave around

seven. So a little after that, unless the traffic is bad."

"I'll be ready. I'm glad you called because I want to tell you about this idea I have. It's a BFD."

"Does BFD mean what I think it means? I always meant to ask Shura."

"Shura and I agreed never to tell, so you'll just have to keep wondering."

"Okay by me. Wondering about junk is my hobby, of sorts."

"See you tomorrow, Richard. Bye."

"Bye, Amelia."

The next night, at exactly seven-fifteen, the doorbell rang.

Kate bounded over like a happy puppy. "It's the Flinkman, it's the Flinkman!"

"Mom, make her stay back, will you?" I held the doorknob. "She'll knock him over!"

Mom laughed. "Not quite! I think Richard can hold his own!" But she turned to Kate anyway and told her to settle down.

I opened the door and found Richard, along with Mr. C. "Hey, look Mom, we got two birds on one ring!"

"Come in, gentlemen!" said Mom happily. I noticed how she brightened at the sight of Mr. C.

"I was fortunate enough to run into my favorite Shakespeareophile making a wish on everyone's favorite Tiki out front," said Mr. C.

"Hey, don't give me away." Richard looked sheepishly at me. "Now she's going to want to know what I was wishing for."

"Let her wonder, Richard, a sense of wonderment is an important thing." Mr. C. turned toward Mom and kissed her cheek. "Don't you agree, Frances?"

"Absolutely." She put her arm around him. "I wonder how I ever got so lucky to find you."

"And if I don't hurry, my parents will wonder where I am," said Richard. "Then the next step will be to send out a search party to locate me, the only Flink son and heir, so we had better make haste, Amelia."

Richard shook Mr. C.'s hand. "Good night, sir, it was nice to see you again."

"You have her home at a reasonable time, Richard, okay? Otherwise her mother and I will be sending out that search party."

I stopped halfway out the door. It was the first time a man had given fatherly instruction for me. I walked back to Mr. C.

"Thank you for that," I whispered as I hugged him. Mom had tears in her eyes, too.

"My pleasure," he said simply.

"Welp! That sounds like a dad if I ever heard one!" said Kate from her perch on the arm of the couch. "Yep, it sure does. Only daddies do that kind of stuff."

"Dum, dum, te, dum. Dum, dum, te dum . . ."
sang Richard.

"Out, out damned spot!" cried Mom as she playfully shoved us outside.

"I'm available to sing at weddings!" called Richard through the closed door. We could hear the laughter inside.

On the way out, just past the Tiki, Richard held my hand. All the way to the car.

The drive through the dusky evening was especially nice since we took Mt. Hollywood Drive through Griffith Park. Slowly we wended our way to the top of the hill. The observatory stood with its round, copper dome just beyond us. The lights of Los Angeles twinkled in the distance.

"Sometimes, from far away, it does look like the City of Angels, doesn't it?" asked Mrs. Flink.

"Indeed it does, my dear," said Mr. Flink, who was an older version of Richard. "Imagine what it looked like to the first people who settled here."

"Must have been dark," said Richard.

His father rolled his eyes.

"Listen, Dad, we're going to the Laserium show, and there's usually a big line. Where do you want to meet?"

"Your mother and I will be seeing the show in the Planetarium Theatre, and it takes at least an hour. Why don't we meet at the Foucault Pendulum in the center of the rotunda, just inside the entrance, around nine."

"Okay." Richard set the little timer on his watch.

While Richard and I waited for our show to start, we strolled around the grounds. I explained my book project to him.

"Wow, I think that's an amazing thing to do! But I see one problem," he said seriously.

"What? I need all the advice I can get!"

"Why would you just talk to girls? Don't you know that guys feel the same kind of stuff?"

"No, I didn't. Not really."

"Well, take it from this duckling's bill," he looked at me, then found something fascinating on the ground to stare at before he continued, "ugly duck- lings come in all shapes, sizes, and sexes."

"You think I should talk to some boys, too?"

"No. I think I should talk to them. I want to help. Besides, they wouldn't tell you anything. Just like a girl probably wouldn't tell stuff to a guy."

"Okay! I'd love for you to help. I'm glad you don't think it's a geeky thing to do."

"Takes a geeky to know a geeky, I guess," he said with a laugh.

"You're not a geek."

He smiled at me and looked out at the lights of the city below. "Well, as the Bard said, 'The world is still deceived with ornament.'"

"Let's go see the light show, Richard," I suggested softly.

"Okay." He took my hand again. "Did you ever notice, Amelia, that you have to be in the dark for a while before your eyes adjust and you can see all the light?"

"Yes, Richard, I have noticed."

We walked, hand-in-hand, into the observatory.

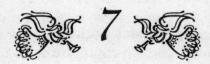

7

Interviewing the girls was much easier than I thought it would be. They were dying to tell someone how they felt. Someone who understood.

That someone was me.

First I met with Luana Gleeson. We took the bus down to Greenblatt's Deli on Sunset Boulevard one Saturday afternoon. I asked for a table in the upstairs dining room so we could watch life on the Sunset Strip below.

"I'll have a pastrami on rye, please," said Lu to our crusty seventy-year-old waiter, Sol.

"Yeah, yeah, and what for you?" he growled at me, licking the tip of his pencil.

"Lox and a bagel, and iced tea."

"Iced tea over here, too," said Lu.

"What am I a dreidel, that I should have to spin

around and around for you girls? No more addi-
tions now. I am bringink what I have written." He
shuffled off.

"He's cheery," said Lu with a giggle.

"He's always like that. He likes to give people a
hard time. But, you'll see, he'll bring your iced tea.
My mom loves to come here just to see Sol. He's
real sweet to my little sister. He likes to grab her
cheeks and call her dumplink."

"She must be cute."

"As a button," I said.

Lu nodded and sighed. "Which brings us to those
of us who aren't."

Sol came over and dumped two iced tea glasses
on the table. They sloshed half their contents onto
the Formica-topped table.

"Thanks," we chimed.

"Enjoy," he grumbled.

"So," I said as I ripped open a pink packet of
sweetener, "maybe to start with, you could tell me
how you feel about your looks and how other kids
have reacted to you."

"Sure. You could call my section of the book 'Q-
Tip.' I've been called that since third grade, so I
guess that's the main reaction of other kids. I *am*
my looks—at least to them."

"I've been called Fleabag a lot," I offered, so she
would know she wasn't alone.

"Fleabag? That's charming. Where do they get

these names? Maybe that's what they do at all those parties we're not invited to. You know, think up names for the third tier."

"Third tier?"

"I made that up." She smiled and explained. "It means that the most popular couple at a school are like the two little people on the top of a wedding cake. They are the cutest, are dressed the best, and everybody wants to be near them. Now, all their friends are one tier lower. Then, holding up the whole cake, is the third tier—you, me, and everybody else."

"Oh, I get it."

"I've had plenty of time to figure it all out." She stirred sugar into her tea and stared out the window. "I guess you could say that I'm someone who is not pretty, who knows it, and who has stopped wishing for miracles. I don't like it, but I accept it."

I got out my notebook and scribbled.

An hour later I had four pages of notes and a half-eaten bagel.

"Geez, I can't believe how I've been running off at the mouth," Lu said. "It's like some kind of weight was lifted off my back or something."

"I know just what you mean," I said, draining my second glass of tea. "If you're like me, you shove this stuff in an old sack and drag it around."

"Yeah, but the old sack gets full after a while," she said.

66

"Yep. And heavy. I hope we can at least make it easier to carry."

"Do you think you can do this? I mean, get it published and everything?" She counted out a few dollars for her share of the check.

"I really do, Lu. I don't think it's impossible."

"Maybe you're right. You did get yourself on the 'Candy K. Crowley Show.' "

"I did, didn't I?" I smiled and dug out a tip for old Sol.

"So, who's next?"

"I asked Brenda, that kind of heavyset girl from our P.E. class. She said she'd like to do it. And I asked a girl from my sewing class named Carol Duffy."

Luana grabbed my arm. "Hey! Have you talked to Cherise Davis?"

"No. I don't even know her."

"Oh!" She hit palm to forehead. "That's right, she's home-schooled now."

"Why?"

"Well, she has this really severe birthmark. I think it's called a wine mark, or something. She has this huge, dark patch covering half her face. It looks like wine spilled all over her and stained her face."

"Is that why she's home?"

"I'm pretty sure. Kids were really hard on her, and I think she didn't want to deal with junior high *and* her face. Kind of a double-whammy. I have her number if you want it."

We walked out into the glare of the California sun and headed for the bus stop.

"I think maybe I will call Cherise," I said as my bus pulled up. Luana scribbled the number on my palm. "Thanks a lot, Lu."

"Thank you!" she called as the doors closed behind me.

That night over dinner I told Mom, Mr. C., and Kate all about my book.

"You are so smart, Melia," said Kate. "I think you're cool."

I smiled and tweaked her nose.

"I think it is a wonderful idea whether it gets published or not," said Mom. "I think you're doing such a worthwhile thing."

"Thanks, Mom."

"And I have something to offer," said Mr. C. "I think it would be good if you took my tape recorder along from now on. That way people can concentrate on what they're saying and not worry about you catching every word."

"Wow! Thanks a lot! My hand was getting cramped trying to write everything down." I looked around the table. "I'm glad nobody said this was a dumb idea. Or said that I couldn't do it."

"Most people can do more than they'd ever

dream," said Mr. C. "And dreams are free. You just have to dream them."

Mom squeezed his hand, and that's when I saw the ring. "Oh wow! You're getting married!" I jumped up and smacked right into Kate, who had catapulted from her chair.

"Took you long enough to notice," said Mr. C. with a rich laugh. "What are you guys, blind?"

My meeting with Brenda the next weekend was an education. I never thought much about being fat because I didn't have to deal with it.

Brenda had to deal with it every day.

I met her at her house.

"Hi, Amelia, come on in!" Brenda opened the door with a big smile. "Come on back to my room; we can talk there."

I followed her down a carpeted hallway and into what, to my eyes, was the perfect bedroom. Brenda had a canopied bed with a flowered coverlet that matched the canopy and the curtains. Her furniture was white, and the carpet was the color of pale pink roses.

"Wow." I breathed the word.

"It is pretty, isn't it?" She gestured at a chair and settled herself on the edge of the bed.

"It really is. If I had to wish for a bedroom, this would be it."

"Thanks. I decorated it myself." She looked around and laughed. "My dad paid for it, though!"

"Good thing, too," I said, "it would take an awful lot of allowance to manage this!"

"Yeah, a lifetime's worth."

We each stared awkwardly around the room for a few minutes. This wasn't the easiest subject to launch into.

"Well, ah, I'm glad you wanted to talk to me," I began, "and I'm glad you didn't feel bad that I asked you."

"Listen, girl, I know I'm fat. It's not something you can really overlook." She smiled and I realized how pretty her face was. Her skin was smooth and clear, not a pimple in sight; and her eyes were dark, almond-shaped, and fringed with black lashes.

I had heard that overweight girls hate to be told that they had "such pretty faces . . . if only you'd lose weight!" So I didn't say that.

"Have you always been chubby?" I asked diplomatically (I hoped).

"Sure have." She pulled a photo album from the drawer in her nightstand. "Here, I thought you might want to see some old pictures of me as I grew up . . ."

I took it.

"And out," she added.

As I turned the pages, I noticed that as she went

from fat little girl to fat big girl, Brenda was always smiling. She looked like the happiest person ever!

"Brenda, you know, you look so happy here. But on the phone you said you've had an awful time because of your looks."

"Let me tell you something about that," she sat up and took the album back and started to speak about a mile a minute.

"Wait a sec. Do you mind if I turn on this tape recorder first?"

"No, that's fine with me." She waited while I got it going. Then she continued: "When you're fat you wake up every morning in this big body, and you know that no matter how nice your hair looks, or how nice your clothes are, or how pretty your things are, that you are nothing more than a huge target. I might as well have black circles painted on my back. There is no hiding! People notice fat first. Then they don't bother with any other part of you."

"I didn't think of it like that."

"Of course not. You're lucky enough to be skinny."

"Maybe, but there are so many other things I don't like about my looks and my body."

"Yeah, but Amelia, you don't understand yet." Her eyes welled up. "It's always open season on fat people. We're hunted all year, and we can't hide.

There is no makeup, no contact lenses, no dress, no hairstyle that I can hide behind."

"It must be awful to have to take showers at school, then. I mean, even more awful than it is for everyone else."

"That's when I hate myself the most," she whispered. "I want to die."

Suddenly I felt my angel nearby. I was getting good at sensing her. I heard Lily's voice inside my head. She said, "Turn off the taping machine and comfort her."

I turned off the tape recorder and sat next to Brenda. I put my arm around her and let her cry. I realized how hard she must work at smiling all the time.

She smiled so people would like her, but nobody ever looked past the fat.

Or the smile.

"When we first moved here, in fifth grade, my mom gave a birthday party for me." She sat up and blew her nose. "I took the invitations to school and everyone said they could come. But on the day of the party, no one did."

"Oh, no."

"I sat in my pink party dress for two hours." She shrugged. "Mostly it was bad for my parents. I think it's hard to have an unpopular kid. So I never told them what I found on the front porch the next day."

"What?"

"A stuffed pig."

I groaned.

"Yeah. Nice touch, huh? The card said, 'We don't party with Miss Piggy.' "

"Brenda, I know this is hard to talk about, but I think other kids should know this stuff."

She nodded.

"So, if you could tell other people something about how you feel about things like that, what would it be?"

She ran her hands through her thick black hair and stared out the window. "I guess I'd like to ask them something, not tell them anything."

I flipped the recorder back on. "Go ahead."

"Do they want to hurt me because, on the outside, I'm ugly? Or because, on the inside, they are?"

I waited. I had a feeling she wasn't done.

"You know what, Amelia? It's much harder being fat than anything."

"Really?"

"Sure. People don't say racist or sexist stuff much anymore, at least not right in your face, but 'fatty,' 'lard-butt,' and 'blubber,' those are all okay."

I didn't say anything.

I didn't know what to say.

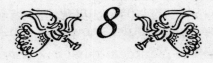

When I got home from Brenda's house, I called Cherise Davis. I had been putting it off because I didn't know her, and I thought the whole thing might be too uncomfortable for both of us.

But something kept reminding me of her.

I decided to talk to her mom first, and explain who I was and what I was doing.

Her mother listened patiently to my spiel, then said, "I don't think it would be a good idea for you to speak to my daughter."

"But, Mrs. Davis," I said, "maybe it would be good for her to talk to someone instead of being home all by herself. And, if she wants, I wouldn't have to use her real name in the book."

"No, I just think it would be a bad idea. The last

thing she needs right now is to be included in a book all about unattractive girls."

"But that's *not* what it's about at all! I'm going to call it *Swan Songs* because everybody in it is really like a swan in hiding."

"No. I'm sorry, dear. But good luck on your project, anyway. Good-bye."

"Wait! Please! Would you just take my name and number, in case she wants to talk?"

"All right. But don't get your hopes up."

"I won't." I gave her the information.

"Good-bye, then."

Click.

I cradled the phone for a minute, then hung up.

"Don't give up on her," said Lily. "Cherise needs this. She needs you."

"I don't see how I can possibly do it if she won't even—"

"That is your first mistake." She smiled and faded as Kate came crashing into the room followed by Cyril, whom Kate rarely mentioned anymore.

"Amelia! Come on! The Flinkman is here to talk to you about stuff for your book, and Mom and Mr. C. want to hear about it. And me, too." She sucked in a breath and rushed on, "And also, we're going to have a special dessert that Mr. C. made."

"What is it?"

"He brought over this pot, and you melt chocolate in it, and then you put stuff on these little stabbers and you dunk them in the chocolate."

"A fondue pot? Yum. I'll be right out."

Kate disappeared and Lily reappeared.

"One more thing, Amelia," she said as I brushed my hair.

"Yes?"

"Remember as you do this book to use a light touch."

"What do you mean?" I stopped brushing and looked at her reflection.

"It shouldn't be too serious or too sad. It should be hopeful." She rose slowly until she hovered near the ceiling of our bedroom. "Hope is light."

"I get it," I said with a smile.

"Do you know why angels can fly, Amelia?"

"Why?"

"Because we take ourselves lightly!" Her laughter tinkled down on me and she disappeared.

I took a smile with me into the living room.

"Hey, Amelia Bedelia!" Richard waved some paper in my direction. "Here are the results of my in-depth research."

"Come and sit down, everyone," called Mom from the kitchen table. "We all want to hear how the book is coming along while we dip into Noel's pot of chocolate."

The rich, dark liquid bubbled gently from the pot

in the middle of the table. Surrounding it were plates of strawberries, bananas, cubed pound cake, mandarin orange sections, and maraschino cherries. We each commandeered a skewer and started stabbing.

"This is my favorite dessert, and not just because of how it tastes," said Mr. C.

"Then why, Daddy?" asked Kate. She had started calling him that as soon as she heard about the wedding. Mr. C. glowed each time she said it.

"Because, little daughter, when I was small my mother wouldn't let me handle anything sharp." He jabbed his skewer into the air for emphasis and laughed. "Beware the blind man with the sharp instrument!"

"I'm more nervous around guys with sharp instruments who can see!" said Richard.

"I second that," said Mom.

"I third it," said Kate with a wave of her skewer. "Even though I don't know what in the heck you guys are talking about."

"Ah, the faith of the young when faced with the unknown," said Mr. C. "Speaking of youth facing the unknown, how is the book project coming along?"

I filled everybody in on my interviews. Then I turned to Richard. "What about you, Richard? What are the guys saying?"

"Just a second," he said through chocolate lips.

"Let me swallow this cake." He gulped and began: "First off, they were easy to locate, since nerds of a feather flock together."

He waited for the groans to die down.

"I have approached some Prince Charmless chaps, and they agree that although good looks are not their strong suit, they don't think it will doom them or anything."

"Really? That's weird." I dunked a strawberry and waited for him to go on. "The girls aren't just bugged by it, they're crushed."

"Bugged is probably a good description of how I feel, too. But not a crushed bug." Richard stopped and thought for a minute. "I've been called names by other guys and taunted in P.E. for my lack of ability concerning any game that involves a ball and no brain, but I guess I handled it by concentrating my efforts on reading and chess and things like that."

"The girls don't take it quite as . . . lightly," I said.

"That's not surprising," offered Mr. C. "Girls are accepted based more on their physical appearance than boys are."

"That's just what one guy in my chess club said," agreed Richard. "He mentioned that there are plenty of geeky guy role models, so we can see that there is life after geekdom."

"Like who?" asked Kate.

"Like Woody Allen. He's made being a geeky guy almost cool. And then there's my personal idol, Steven Spielberg. He's often talked about how he was a geek all through school, so he turned to making movies even back then."

"And what about Bill Gates?" said Mom. "I was just reading about him. He's the president of Microsoft, and one of the richest men in the country; he was a computer nerd all through school."

"Being a nerd can pay off," said Kate. "I saw an after-school special about it."

"Pay off if you're a guy," I added. "I can't think of too many role models like that for girls. All we have stuck in our faces are gorgeous, skinny models and those two old ladies on the supreme court."

Mr. C. laughed. "I'm sure Justices O'Connor and Ginsberg would cringe at that."

"You know what I mean," I said. "I don't think girls see them as big role models or anything."

"That's true," said Mom. "In fact, you hardly see them at all."

"It's the robes," said Richard.

Mr. C. laughed. "You're quick, Richard. Quicker than me!"

"Okay, okay, you two," admonished Mom with a smile. "Enough. What about the rest of the boys you talked to, Richard?"

"Well, there were some cool stories about dissatisfaction with physical traits. Like, one guy slept with a clothespin on his nose every night for a year, hoping to make his nostrils smaller. And another guy tried to stretch himself taller by hanging like a bat in his closet. Guys are very inventive."

Everybody laughed.

"This whole thing reminds me of *The Enchanted Cottage*," said Mom.

"Is that an old movie?" I asked.

She nodded.

I turned to Richard and explained, "Mom knows old movies like you know Shakespeare. Go ahead, Mom."

"It's this lovely old movie with Robert Young and Dorothy McGuire. He was disfigured in the war and she is unattractive, or thinks she is, and they come together through their feelings of ugliness. Then they get married. They move into this lovely little cottage, and whenever they are in the cottage, they appear beautiful."

"The house makes them pretty?" asked Kate.

"No, honey, they just think it does. They look pretty because they are seeing each other through the eyes of love."

"Oh, rent that one for us, Mom," Kate said.

"Yeah, then tell me where that cottage is," I added.

"I haven't even told you the best part," she continued. "The only one who understands what is happening is their neighbor."

"Is he psychic?" asked Richard with a large grin.

"No." Mom looked at Mr. C. "He's blind."

"Why are you all looking so surprised?" asked Mr. C. "If you want to know who is truly beautiful, ask a blind man. For only the blind can see the beauty of the soul."

"Shakespeare?" asked Richard.

"Nope. Christopher," he replied with a huge grin. "You know, I've always thought that they should have blind people judge beauty pageants. It would be more accurate."

"Yeah, then maybe I'd have a chance at the crown," deadpanned Richard.

Laughter circled the table.

I decided, then and there, that I would find a way to get to Cherise Davis, who was locked up in an unenchanted cottage.

A tingle began at the top of my head and traveled down to my toes. That was Lily's sign that I was on the right track.

The phone rang and Kate flung herself at it.

"Amelia, it's for you. It's a girl with a real pretty name."

"Who?"

"Cherise Davis."

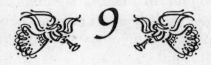

9

"What are you wearing to school today, Amelia?" Kate's voice came to me from inside our closet.

"I dunno. How hot is it?"

"Medium. But that's not why I asked." She brought out three different blouses and held them up in front of her.

"Why'd you ask then?"

"It's picture day. Usually you don't like that day, and you hate whatever you decided to wear." She slipped on her favorite pink blouse and smiled at herself.

I groaned and fell back on my bed. "I forgot. I was too busy thinking about interviewing Cherise after school today." I got up, dragged myself over to the closet, and scanned my suddenly inadequate wardrobe.

"Well, I'm all ready." She slid a pink and white headband into her hair. "I'm gonna go eat my cereal." She paused in the doorway. "Wear your red sweater. It's happy."

"I look like an apple in that!" I called after her.

"Okay. Then you'll look like a happy apple," she replied.

I yanked the sweater over my head and went to work on my hair.

It's amazing what you *can't* do with fine, thin hair. And perms cost fifty dollars, which put them way out of my league!

With all this talk about inner beauty, you'd think I would lighten up, I thought grumpily.

"Yes, indeed, I would have thought so, too," said Lily. .

"I know. I know." I set the brush down and turned to her. "Shura used to give me the hardest time about this kind of thing."

"Did you think Shura was pretty, Amelia?" Lily fiddled with the jars of makeup on my dresser.

"Oh, yes. She was really pretty. I heard people say she was striking."

"Was she skinny?"

"No. Shura was big and healthy. She used to say that Russians didn't come in small." I smiled at the memory.

"What about her eyes?"

"They were green and kind of close-set, like Bar-bra Streisand's."

"And her nose? Was it small and perky? Like the nose you want?"

"No-o-o. It was kind of medium big, and it had a little bump on the bridge from when she fell off the swings in second grade."

"But she was beautiful?"

"Yes." I watched as Lily put blush on her face. It looked funny, somehow.

"How could she have been beautiful, Amelia? The person you described is heavy, with a big bumpy nose, and odd eyes."

"But she *was*!" My eyes welled up.

Lily slipped a weightless arm around my shoulders. "I know she was," she said. "Now go and have your picture taken. And remember your best friend."

When they took our pictures during P.E. later that day, I did something new. When I sat down I looked right at the photographer, pushed my glasses up, threw him a grin as if it were a handful of confetti, and thought to myself, BFD! It's picture day!

I have a feeling that this year they'll turn out pretty . . . good. Pretty good.

After school I went straight to Cherise's house.

Her mother opened the door and smiled. "You

must be Amelia," she said. "I'm so happy that you've come."

"Yes, ma'am." I followed her inside the cheery house. Everything was done in pale yellow and white. Somehow I had expected it to be all dark and foreboding.

"I hope you didn't think me rude when we spoke on the phone." She gestured at a flowered couch and I sat down.

"No, I thought you were nice. Just concerned, I guess."

"I am. I feel so protective of Cherise. I don't want her to be hurt anymore." She went over to the hallway and called for Cherise to come out. "But when I told her about you and your book, she was very excited. I guess it never occurred to me that she might want to air her feelings in public about these kind of . . . things."

I nodded. Boy, I was nervous. Where should I look when she came out? How could I be sure not to stare?

And then she was there.

Cherise Davis was a little shorter than me, with heavy, honey-blond hair that she wore in a simple, long bob with bangs. Her eyes were a light, corn-flower blue and she had double dimples.

And across one side of her face was a large, slightly raised, almost purple birthmark. It ran from her chin to her forehead, and seemed as if it could seep over to the other side of her face at any moment.

"Cherise, this is Amelia," said her mother. "Amelia, this is my daughter, Cherise."

"Hi, Amelia." Cherise turned her "good" side toward me and sat on the couch. "I'm glad you could come over. And see me." She turned halfway and half-smiled.

"Hey, Cherise. Gee, your house is so pretty . . . and so are you." I hadn't planned to say that last part, but it slipped out.

Her mom retreated to the kitchen and we were alone.

"So," I said with a sigh. "I guess your mom told you the details of what I'm doing."

"Yes, and I thought it was dumb at first. But the more I thought about it, the more I had this weird feeling that maybe I had something to say." She folded her hands on her lap. "So that's when I called you to come over, before I chickened out."

"I'm glad you didn't."

"Me, too. So far."

We laughed and the stiffness bent a bit.

"Um, Cherise, first, could you tell me what the name is of what you have on your, ah, cheek? Is it a birthmark?" I clicked on the tape recorder.

"It's called a Port-Wine Stain," she said. "And it

86

is a birthmark. It's permanent, and as you saw, it takes up almost half of my face."

"Couldn't it be removed?"

"Well, some of them can, but ones like mine can't. They're too big, and it would affect my eye and nose; and there would be a lot of scarring. So I have to live with it. They can fade them some, and you can wear makeup, but it doesn't disappear." Her hand went to her cheek.

"What's it like?" I wished I had said that in a nicer way, but that's how it came out. So I just waited.

"It's pretty bad sometimes. Embarrassing. But it's definitely worse now that I'm older. When I was little I got sort of used to kids staring at me, and we lived in a smaller town then, so it was easier."

"Fewer people to stare?"

"That, and I guess people got used to how I looked, and they pretty much left me alone. Then we moved here in fifth grade."

"And it got worse?"

"Yeah. For some reason it seems that bigger groups of kids are meaner. I don't know why. They just wouldn't let up, all through fifth and sixth grades. It just wore me out; the names, and the constant teasing. Their favorite name for me was Phantom of the Opera."

"Did you have any friends at school?"

"Yes. I had a few, but they couldn't protect me. You know how school is."

"I know. Sometimes, you really want to stand up for other kids, but you're afraid that the in-crowd will attack you if you do."

"So this year I asked if I could be home-schooled, and my parents said okay. And here I am."

"Are you going to be home forever, though? I mean, don't you want to come out? Don't you want to go to junior high and high school with other kids?"

"Not really. Would you?" She turned toward me. "Be honest."

"I don't know. I think I'd get lonely being at home all the time."

"Home isn't lonely. School was lonely. I was like the one burnt cookie in a perfect batch. Who wants that one?"

I had no answer for her.

The tape recorder hummed and their grandfather clock bonged.

"You know what this reminds me of?" I asked.

"What?"

"It reminds me of this old movie star named Mary Pickford." A tingle went up and down my spine, so I continued: "She was considered to be just about the prettiest girl in the whole country, but when she got older, she hated her aging face so much that she hid in her house and wouldn't come out."

"That could be me," she whispered. Then Cherise turned completely toward me. "What ever happened to her?"

"She died in that house—at Pickfair. People who came to visit her could only talk to her from a phone in the hall. Only her husband could see her, and not even him all the time."

"Oh." Cherise turned off the recorder. "Do you think I'll end up like that?"

"I don't know, but you could I guess. I mean, if you never come out."

I saw Lily hovering near the piano. She gestured at the newspaper on the piano bench. I went over and got it. It was opened to the Calendar section of the *L.A. Times*. And right there, on the front, was Pickfair.

"Hey, look at this, Cherise!" I took the paper to her. "They're having tours at Mary's old house, Pickfair, this weekend!"

"Oh, look at it, it's like a castle almost."

"It says here it's finally been refurbished and opened to the public. It's just like it was in the twenties, and there's all sorts of stuff from Mary Pickford's life and career that you can look at."

I felt Lily poke me.

"You wanna go with me?" I asked with a giant leap of faith.

Cherise didn't miss a beat. "Yes, I do want to go."

I grinned. "It's a date." I turned the recorder back on. "It's a date, right? Say it so I have proof."

"It's a date," she said with a nervous laugh. "I promise. I think."

"This will be so cool." I smiled at her encouragingly. "One last thing, Cherise, could you share some feeling you have about your looks?"

"I thought about this after I first agreed to talk with you for the book, and I guess I can explain it best by saying that my favorite day of the year is not Christmas, like for most kids. Mine is Halloween."

"Why?"

"Because on Halloween I get to wear a mask, and for one night I'm just like everyone else."

"And your worst day?"

"Picture day. What else?"

I turned the machine off and hugged her.

10

Mrs. Davis stood in the doorway, wringing her hands.

"Bye, Mom. Don't worry, I'll be okay," called Cherise from our car.

"I know," squeaked her mother.

"She looks as if she needs one more hug," suggested my mom, who was driving. The world's biggest old-movie fan was not going to miss a trip to Pickfair!

Cherise hopped out and ran over to her mom. Mrs. Davis mouthed "Thank you" to us over her daughter's shoulder.

Mom smiled and honked, and Cherise came running back and squeezed into the backseat of the vee dub. "Thanks for waiting, Mrs. Fleeman," she said.

"No problem. I understand completely, Cherise. It's a Mom thing."

We chugged down the hill and I asked Mom where Kate was.

"I sent her over to Noel's house to help stuff the invitations. Oh, did I tell you? We're going to be married there, in the living room."

"That will be neat." Mr. C. lived with his sister and her husband in a real nice house in the Hollywood Hills. I explained to Cherise about Mom and Mr. C. getting married.

"Congratulations," she said. "I love weddings."

"I hope you'll come, Cherise," said Mom. "We'd like to have you."

"Maybe I will . . . I'm not sure." Cherise put her hand to her face and looked out the window.

Lily whispered something in my ear and I listened carefully.

"Mom and I and my little sister are going shopping for the wedding dress in a couple weeks," I said. "Wouldn't you like to come along? Those dresses are so much fun to look at. And since we'll be with Mom, those old ladies in the bridal department will have to let us look at everything! We can ignore their sour looks!"

Mom laughed. "I am looking forward to that! We should go to lunch, too. Make a day of it."

"I'd love that," said Cherise. "I'd really love it."

"I hope you can come, dear," said Mom.

"We'll see," she replied. "Maybe by then I'll be ready."

"Hey! There it is!" I squealed as we turned off Benedict Canyon and climbed up Summit Drive. "I can see the turrets!"

"I don't know if those are turrets," said Mom with a laugh.

"Oh, whatever, then!" I hung my head out the window and pointed. "Look at that on the gate! A big letter *P* is scrolled into the ironwork at the top! Neat!"

We got into a long line of cars and waited our turn to park.

"I thought maybe there would be only old people here," I observed, "but there are all sorts of ages."

"Yes," said Mom. "More people are interested nowadays. They show silent movies on cable now, and the revival houses have been running the silents for ages. They really are an important part of cinematic history."

"And I guess Mary Pickford was the biggest star of all back in those days. Right, Mom?"

"Absolutely. She, Douglas Fairbanks, and Charlie Chaplin were the biggest stars in the world because silent films could be seen by everyone—there was no language barrier."

"Everybody understands a look," said Cherise.

"They certainly do," said Mom. "Oh, look, we can park here and get tickets at the gate from that man who is dressed up as Chaplin!"

A small, mustached man dressed like the famous little tramp welcomed us and directed us to our tour guide.

We entered through ornate doors and found ourselves in a large, tiled foyer. A stairway rose in front of us and massive windows offered a view of the sloping backyard, and its pool beyond.

"This is the home of Mary Pickford, America's Sweetheart," said the guide with a sweeping gesture. "She was born Gladys Mary Smith in Toronto, Canada, on April 8, 1893. She went on to become the most famous woman in the world, and a successful business woman who helped create the movie company, United Artists . . ."

As the guide rambled on, I scanned the crowd. A few people had stared at Cherise, but mostly they paid attention to the beautiful house and all its memorabilia.

Halfway through the tour, I glanced through a half-closed door and saw Lily. She motioned at me to come to her. I hung back from the rest of the group and slipped through the door.

An old man sat at a desk, signing papers. Lily nodded toward him. I walked over the heavy oriental carpet until I stood before him. All of my reading about Hollywood history came back to me. I knew this face. It was Buddy Rogers, Mary's last husband, and a movie star himself.

He looked up.

"Are you Buddy Rogers? The movie star?"

The old movie star in him came alive. He stood, straightened his tie, smiled a still-a-star smile, and extended a somewhat shaky hand. "Why, yes, my dear, I am. How on earth would you know that?"

"I love old movies and their history," I explained. "And I just loved Mary."

"Didn't we all?"

I nodded.

"I'm just signing a few tour programs, would you like one?"

Lily shook her head and made the motion of a book. I understood.

"No, thank you, sir. What I would really like is to ask you a few things about Mary."

"Certainly. The 'Little Girl with the Curls,' that's how Mary was known." He seemed to drift off into his past. "America's sweetheart she was, and will always be."

I told him I agreed and then explained to him the story of my ugly duckling book, and my interest in Mary's last, hidden years.

"That is true. I tried to convince her otherwise,

but she insisted that no one would want to look at her when she grew old. She even made me remove all the mirrors from the house."

"That story has always made me so sad," I said. "Couldn't she have been, I don't know, America's sweet grandma, or something?"

He smiled. "No, she wanted only to stay beautiful forever." He looked up with watery, old eyes. "She didn't know she was beautiful. Forever."

"Could I tell her story in my book?" I asked.

"If you think it would help," he said. He walked over to some photographs on the wall and gazed at them. "Tell them how, when she was a little girl in Toronto, she would eat rose petals."

"Why did she—"

"Because, even then, she thought she wasn't pretty enough. So she ate the flowers hoping their beauty would grow in her. Please, tell them that. Maybe then they will understand."

Lily hovered near him and kissed his cheek. He smiled and said, "I can still feel Mary here. Yes, I am not alone."

"Thank you, sir, thank you very much. I'll send you one of my books if I ever get it published. I promise."

"Not if, my dear," he said, sitting down at his desk. "When."

I backed out of the room and tried to pull myself

together in the hall outside his door. Lily appeared next to me.

"He's an old sweetie," I said. "But it was kind of sad."

"Life can be sad," she said. "Angels can only try to help. If Mary had listened to me, she could have been happier."

"Listened to you?"

"Yes. I was her guardian angel. But I could never get her to hear me."

My mouth hung open.

"Surprised?" She laughed. "I never give up. I couldn't reach her, but I reached you. Why do you think you've always been so interested in her?"

"Boy, Lily, you are . . ." I shook my head and looked into her eyes.

"What?"

"Miraculous."

"I have a secret for you . . . everyone is." She waved her arm over her head, with a knowing smile, and disappeared.

I got off the bus and walked to Richard's house. My backpack was heavy with my handwritten manuscript. Here it was, almost December, and the book was ready to be put on the computer and edited by Mrs. Flink.

Twenty girls had talked to me. Word seemed to

spread and one person would lead to another. By last week I was having to turn people away.

The book had almost seemed to write itself. Actually, I guess each girl kind of wrote her own piece; I just put it together. I rang the Flink's doorbell.

Thanks, I whispered to Lily as I waited. Even if it never gets published, it has been great for all of us.

"Hey, Amelia Bedelia! Come on in! Dad has the computer all set up for us. Let's hit it!" Richard grabbed my arm and dragged me into the house. His enthusiasm for the book was as great as mine.

"Remember, I hardly know how to use a computer," I warned. "You know how it is at school; they don't have that many, and there is always a line a mile long to get on one."

"It's easy! Here, sit down, and I'll teach you all about the amazing world of the PC."

"Okay, just go slow. I'll get it better if you don't rush through it. I have a feeling it will be just like math. I'm okay with it if the teacher goes slow and doesn't act like I'm dumb if I ask a lot of questions." I sat down and stared at the little blinking square—the cursor—I remembered.

"Ask away. Ask any question you want. I want to be a teacher someday, you know. You'll be good practice."

"Thanks. I've always wanted to be a guinea pig! Just go easy on me at first."

"To quote Othello, 'Those that do teach young babes, do it with gentle means and easy tasks.' "

"Sounds good to me." I leaned forward and stared at the menu on the screen.

"Hey, lean back, it's bad for your eyes that way. And besides, my dad hates drool in the keyboard."

I laughed. "Okay, okay. Where do we start?"

"Well, Dad has set it up for manuscript format, all we have to do is pull it all together and break it into chapters. Then we can spell-check, which is the greatest invention since Cliff Notes."

We leaned in toward the screen at the same moment and cracked our heads together.

Richard rubbed his head and smiled. "Well, two heads are better than one!"

I groaned and shook my head at him and the joke.

I heard Lily giggling in my left ear.

Three heads, I thought to myself. We have three heads here.

11

The bell rang and I packed up my English book. I slid out of my desk and headed for the door.

"Wait, Amelia," said Mr. Jacobs.

"Yes?" I shifted my pack anxiously. Did I get a low grade on that last test, I wondered. I had been really busy with the book. . . .

He interrupted my anxiety attack. "Good job on the paper you did for *The Diary of Anne Frank*. I thought it was very perceptive."

"Really? Thanks. I'd already read it before. I guess that helped."

"Could be." He sat on the edge of his desk and smiled. "Listen, I don't want to keep you, but I want you to do something for me."

"Okay. What?"

"I run the drama club after school, and the principal has asked us to do the play version of Anne Frank's diary. It will be an active part of the big holocaust unit we do."

"What does that have to do with me?"

"I want you to try out for the part of Anne."

I stared at him. The words behind his head on the chalkboard went all blurry. "You're kidding me."

"No." He waved his hand. "Now, I don't know that you'll get it for sure, but I think you should try out. You really understand the character, and that's half the battle with acting. What do you say?"

I swallowed. "I say okay. I'll try out."

"Great!" He jumped up and patted my shoulder. "That's great!"

My stomach flipped at the thought. "When will it be?"

"Oh, you have plenty of time. We'll have try outs just after Christmas break; it will take a few weeks to get the cast set, then we'll start putting it on the boards in late January."

I thanked him for asking me and floated home. Would I really get a chance to be an actress?

Dreams of acting abruptly sank as I walked up the street toward our apartment. The manager was out front pulling the Tikis out of the ground and stacking them, like so many logs, on an old truck.

"Hey, Mr. Sanchez, what are you doing to the Tikis?"

"Hi, Amelia. I'm taking the old guys out. The company that owns the building wants to put in a whole new look. And the old Tikis just don't go with the new theme." He smiled sadly and wiped his face with his bandanna.

"My little sister will be so disappointed. She loved these old things." I rubbed one of the Tikis. I realized as I spoke that I would miss them, too. "What's the new theme?"

"It will be called Sun and Sand. Some kind of beach theme. But I guess you won't see it, since your mama tells me you will be moving after the wedding."

"Yeah! We're actually getting a house. I haven't lived in a house before. I'll miss our old apartment."

He laughed. "Oh, you won't miss it for long. Having a house, even a small one, is like having a castle. I love my old house, even though she could use a new roof and all new plumbing."

Just then an idea came out of the blue skies and landed right in my head. I leaned toward Mr. Sanchez and whispered my request in his ear.

"Sí," he said with a chuckle. "I'll do it!"

That night we ate dinner at Greenblatt's Deli and had a family meeting about the wedding, the new house, and how to get my book published.

"Mrs. Flink checked with the company that published her textbook, but they didn't even want to read it."

"Maybe they only do textbooks," said Mr. C.

"I guess. But the man there told her that I would never get published without a literary agent. He said a lot of publishers won't read manuscripts that you just send to them."

Kate sipped her milk. "That's dumb. How's anybody not famous s'posed to do it? And what if they have a real good book?"

Sol came over with a pitcher of milk. "You need more milk, dumplink. It is good for the bones." He refilled her glass.

"You're my pal, Sol," said Kate.

He grinned and looked around the table. "Why so glum here? Usually you have a good time at my place." He leaned toward Mr. C. "I'm pouring more coffee. You wait before you drink. It's very hot."

"Thank you for the warning," said Mr. C.

"So?" Sol stood, a milk pitcher in one hand and a coffee pot in the other. "Where the smiles have gone?"

I explained about my book.

"Okay. I tell you." He placed the containers on the table, pulled out a piece of paper, and scribbled something. "This is the address of my son in New

York City. He works as a lawyer for one of them book houses. He will maybe get it to somebody who reads it and likes it, yes?"

"Oh, Sol, that is so sweet of you," said Mom. "But should we impose?"

"You are not imposing. And I am the father. I don't impose. I ask my son a favor. He does it. That is how it is done."

Mom slipped the paper in her purse and kicked me under the table.

I jumped. "Oh, thank you very much, Sol. I wish I could do something for you."

"No, no. You are a nice kid. You come to my place and bring friends. That's good. I know a good kid when I see one. Now, no more thanking. I'm getting your sandwiches." He nodded at Mom and shuffled off to the kitchen.

"Keep your fingers crossed, everyone," said Mom. "Sol might just be a good-luck charm."

"Good thing we were always nice to him," said Kate.

"Geez, Kate, you don't act nice just to get stuff back. You just act nice just to be nice." I poked her.

"I didn't make up the rules, Melia. I just know how it works." She threw a sugar packet at me. "Nice is like a boomerang. It always comes back. Maybe not the next day or anything, but it comes back. I've been watching. It works."

"Girls, girls," said Mom. "No more arguing, poking, or throwing. We have a wedding and a new house to discuss."

"That's right," said Mr. C. "We've narrowed the houses down to three choices. We want to take you out this weekend to have a look at them. Then we'll decide."

They all started talking at once, and I retreated into my own thoughts. Book, wedding, play, school, the memory of Shura . . .

"Look." Lily's whisper invaded my head.

I glanced out the window and down to the street scene below. There was a girl down there. All alone.

"What?" I asked silently.

"That is your new best friend," replied Lily.

I stared with disbelief. How could Lily be so wrong?

I had seen this girl around school. She was tall, angular, and angry. Her hair was dyed a strange shade of red, and she wore big, ripped jeans and old tee shirts every day. The shirts always bore some kind of message. Today's message was "Authority Sucks."

She hung out with the crowd of kids that I crossed the street to avoid. This . . . creature . . . my next best friend? No way.

Lily's voice came in loud and clear. "Amelia. You

are judging her just as you have been judged. Look beyond what your eyes can see. Tee shirts can be deceptive, as can beauty."

I swallowed a lump in my throat and looked down at the girl. She lit a cigarette and sauntered out of my sight.

Now I remembered: I had seen her in P.E. She was always getting in trouble for not dressing in her gym outfit. Oh, yeah, her name was Slick Jamison.

"I'm supposed to be friends with a person called, Slick?" I asked silently.

"Her real name is Grace," replied Lily evenly. "Speak to the part of her that is Grace."

I groaned and rested my head against the window.

"Are you feeling ill, Amelia?" asked Mr. C.

"Yes. I'm feeling a little sick to my stomach." I sighed. "But it will pass." I straightened up and sipped my water. "I hope."

12

I knew it was the right house as soon as I saw it. So did Kate.

It was white with blue trim, an older house in an older neighborhood. There was a small front yard and a big backyard with a brick patio, and a tree-house platform in an old oak tree.

"This is the one, Daddy, I know it," said Kate as we charged inside and scoped out the bedrooms. "It's perfect. Especially the platform in the tree!" She clanged out the backdoor and made a beeline for the tree.

"Amelia? What do you think?" he asked.

"I love it," I said. "I loved it as soon as we turned onto the street."

The house was on Lily Lane.

"I'm so relieved," said Mom. "I was afraid you'd

each pick a different place, and then one of you would be unhappy for years to come!" She grabbed Mr. C.'s hand and pulled him into the hall. "Oh, Noel, right here is where the other family used to measure their children as they grew. The marks are still on the wall, with their names and the date." She brushed her fingers over it. "How sweet."

He hugged her and said, "Maybe we can add a name to it."

I smiled and left them alone while they kissed.

I joined Kate in the leaves of the tree house.

"Amelia, we won't have to change schools, will we?" She pulled a leaf from above her head and twirled it around.

"No. I asked already. We'll go to the same schools."

"Good. Because I have friends and I don't want to leave them behind. Especially Beth, my first best friend."

"That would be hard to do," I said wistfully. "Really hard. Best friends don't come along every day."

She looked at me, scooted over, and slipped her little arm around my waist. "You still have me," she said quietly. "And now we have Mommy *and* a daddy. And we have a house, and maybe we can have a dog."

I nodded and started to cry. "You're right. I know

I should be grateful, and I am." I wiped the tears away. "But I'll always miss Shura, I guess. She just stays with me like a shadow."

"Maybe she's supposed to."

We stayed up there until they called us. Mom was walking around right underneath us, calling our names.

"Daughters!" called Mr. C. "Come on down from that tree; I can hear you twittering up there."

We smiled at each other.

"Okay, Dad," I said, calling him that for the first time. "We're coming."

December fifth was sunny and cool. Perfect California weather for a wedding.

All the girls that I had interviewed for the book came, even Cherise. Richard was there with his parents, and so were lots of other people from the hospital where Mom worked and from the Bret Harte School.

Things were sure hectic!

"Amelia!" wailed Mom. "Help me with my zipper, it's stuck!"

Aunt Jean, Dad's sister, laughed and fussed over Mom's bouquet. "Fran, you look gorgeous, and that zipper will come up if you just stop fussing at it."

"I know, I know," said Mom. "But I can't help it. I even got a pimple, if you can believe that!"

Aunt Jean patted my back. "I have to go check

on the caterer and the minister. You stay here with the bride, okay?"

"Okay. Will you check on Katie, Aunt Jean? She might be getting her dress dirty or something."

"Will do." She smiled. "It's so nice to have girls around the house! You look so pretty, Amelia!" She swept out of the room.

I looked in the mirror as I zipped Mom. I did look pretty good. For me.

Lily appeared in the far corner and hovered over a high-backed chair. "I love weddings," she said silently to me. "They're so hopeful."

"Weddings are so hopeful, aren't they, Mom?" I said.

"How astute, dear." She fixed her lipstick and fussed with her bangs. "You are so right. Beginnings are hopeful. I'm certainly filled with hope right now." She patted her tummy. "And butterflies."

"But they're hopeful butterflies!" I said.

She laughed and held my hand. "Honey, would you get my purse? I left it on the hall table. My compact is in there."

"Sure."

I went downstairs and was careful not to touch the flowers that were wound around the banister. White ribbons with doves attached were swagged in each doorway, and the choir from Bret Harte

School was singing love songs that wafted through the house along with the fragrance of the flowers.

I stood on the stairs for a minute and looked into the huge living room.

Cherise was talking to some kids, and she wasn't even hiding her face very much. Richard and another guy were checking out Uncle Leo's stereo system. Kate was leading Beth around and showing her the house. People were smiling and chatting.

I breathed in the goodness of my life.

Then the doorbell rang.

No one went for it after it rang again. So I opened the door.

"UPS. Sign here."

I signed and took the package. It was large and heavy and . . . I looked at the return address. It was from the publisher where we had sent the book! We gave them this address since we were in the middle of moving.

It was my book being returned. My mood darkened and my heart went heavy.

I blinked back tears of disappointment and shoved the package into the hall closet. I couldn't let anyone see it. Or my disappointment. Not today. There was more important stuff in the world than this one book.

A tingle went all over me.

Why had I come down here in the first place? Oh, yes, Mom's purse. I grabbed it and ran back up the stairs. My mother needed me.

Half an hour later the tune of "Here Comes the Bride" floated up to us.

"This is it." Mom sighed and gave me a big hug. "I couldn't have done it without you, honey," she said.

"That's okay. You look so pretty, Mom."

We looked at her in the mirror. She was wearing an ivory-colored dress with a sweetheart neck. Tiny beads were sewn into the neckline, and the hem was scalloped with slightly larger beads. Her thick auburn hair was worn in a French twist, and she wore a pillbox hat with a tiny veil.

There was a tap on the door. "Where comes the bride?" asked Uncle Leo, who was going to walk Mom down the aisle.

"Come in, Leo. I'm ready." She smiled at me. "I mean, we're ready."

I squeezed her hand and hurried down the stairs. As the maid of honor, I was to precede her down the aisle.

No one knew it, but Lily walked with me.

After the ceremony Dad requested the quartet to play the first song so that he and Mom could dance.

"Okay, boys, I want to hear, 'Dancing in the Dark,' and I want to hear it loud and clear!"

Everyone laughed and clapped and cried.

It was a great moment.

I soaked up the happiness around me and I felt light.

"Where is Richard Flink?" called Dad after the first dance ended.

"Right here, sir." Richard stepped forward. "What can I do for you?"

"I think a Shakespearean quote would be appropriate right about now. What have you got?"

"I was hoping you'd ask," Richard said with a bow. He cleared his throat. "This is from *A Midsummer Night's Dream:* 'Love looks not with the eyes, but with the mind, and therefore is winged Cupid painted blind.' "

The guests applauded, Dad shook Richard's hand, and then the quartet struck up another song.

Richard asked me to dance.

So did a couple other boys.

I completely forgot how disappointed I was about my book.

Maybe because being happy for someone else is the best cure for the blues.

"It's too bad about your book, honey," said Mom just before Christmas, when I finally told her what had happened. "We'll just have to try some other publisher."

"It's okay. Well, maybe it's not okay, but I don't want to worry about it right now. I feel like if it's meant to be published, then it will be. Besides, look at you, you must feel bad that you can't take a honeymoon trip."

She smiled as she unpacked Kate's Winnie-the-Pooh cup. "Oh, that's not bothering me. We sunk every penny into the house, and it's worth it."

"At least it looks like we'll be unpacked and settled before Christmas. Man, it's taken forever to empty all these boxes."

"Yes, and then we'll just have more to open on Christmas morning!"

"That's different!" I said with a laugh.

The phone rang and I grabbed it.

"Hello?"

"Hi. May I speak to Amelia, please?"

"Yes? This is she."

"Amelia, this is Candy Crowley. Do you remember me?"

"Are you kidding?" My eyes bugged out of my head. "Sure I do! You're the only famous talk show host I've ever known. I'm so surprised that you would call me."

"Surprised? Well, since you mailed me that manuscript of yours, I thought you might be expecting a call. By the way, I love the book!"

"Wait, wait, wait, you have my book?" I clung to the receiver with both hands.

"Yes. You know, *Swan Songs*, dedicated to your friend Shura Najinsky? The one you sent me a few weeks ago?"

I slapped my hand over the mouthpiece. "Mom, did you send my book to the Candy Crowley offices?"

"No. I didn't. What does she want?"

"Um, Miss Crowley, I guess a friend sent it to you, or something, and didn't tell me; but I'm glad they did. And you liked it?"

"No, I loved it." She laughed. "Look, maybe you have someone who is being a secret Christmas elf, or something. Either way, I showed it to some friends I have in publishing, and although they didn't think it would work as a full-length book—"

"Oh, poop."

"Wait now, don't poop out yet. I have a good friend who is starting a new magazine for teenage girls, one that focuses a little less on the outside and more on the inside—"

"And she likes it?" I jumped up and down.

"She does. And she thought she could break it into three parts and run it in her magazine! How's that sound?"

"Fabulous!"

"You're not disappointed that it's not a book?"

"No way! I think it would go great in a magazine."

"I'm glad you think so, because after that I want

to have you and the kids you interviewed as guests on the show."

"*Oh wow!*" I screamed. "*You're kidding!*"

"Amelia!" said Mom. "Tell me what is—"

"Thank you, Miss Crowley, this is beyond anything I had hoped for! Or dreamed of!"

"Hey, thank you. And Merry Christmas, Amelia. I'll call you after the holidays and we'll work out the details. Good-bye!"

I hung up and tried to hug Mom while I jumped around the kitchen and told her what had happened.

After Mom gave me a drink of juice and made me sit down, I said, "Now, who in the world sent that manuscript to Candy Crowley?"

"Who knows?" said Mom. "Maybe you have a guardian angel?"

"Could be," I said. "You never know."

I asked Lily that night.

"No, Amelia, I didn't do it." She smiled and sewed stars to the hem of her gown.

"But you know who did, don't you?"

"Yes. And I'll never tell."

"Why not?"

"Because the boomerang of kindness is simply on its return flight. Flinging the boomerang is what matters, not who flung it."

I gave up.

There is just no arguing with an angel.

13

"Okay, my last present for all of you is outside," I said on Christmas morning after everything had been opened and oohed over.

They looked at me.

"Cool! More stuff!" Kate jumped up. "Where outside?"

"Just follow me. I have it well hidden." We donned our new slippers and robes and trooped outside to the backyard.

I led them to the farthest corner of the yard and pulled the tarp off the present.

"Our Tiki!" yelled Mom and Kate.

Dad laughed. "How in the world?"

"Mr. Sanchez brought it over in his truck. He saved it for me. Then he dragged it back here and laid it behind the bushes so you wouldn't see."

"Is that why you babysat for him two weekends in a row?" asked Mom.

"Yep. We traded."

"Goody!" said Kate. "All we have to do is dig a hole and stand him up, and we'll have good luck again."

"I think we already have it," said Dad.

"Yeah, but it can't hurt," said Kate. "Hey, can we put him in the front yard?"

"*No way, José!*" said our parents in unison.

That night I climbed into bed in my very own room. It was weird not having Kate around. Although, come to think of it, since we'd moved into the house, she had slept in my room about half the time.

I didn't mind.

Lily hovered near the window and stared out at the moonlight. She sighed contentedly and said, "Well, Amelia, it has been quite a time, hasn't it?"

"Yes." I snuggled into my blankets. "I'm so grateful for all the things that have happened to me. The good and the bad. Somehow it all seems to equal a light blue life."

"Indeed," she mused, "our lives are what we color them."

"And I have a lot to look forward to next year," I said. "School, and maybe being in a play, and my friends, and the magazine story, and being on

Candy Crowley again, and this family. . . ."

"And, of course, your plan to get to know Grace Slick Jamison this year." Lily crossed her arms and eyed me angelically.

"I forgot," I said.

"No you didn't."

"Okay. I didn't."

That's another thing you can't do with an angel: lie.

"We're not finished yet, Amelia," she said gleefully. "There are many lost fish in the sea."

"What if I can't find my net?" I asked hopefully.

"Then you'll just have to take the plunge and get all wet!" she replied with that lilting laugh.

I smiled in the dark and turned my face toward the moonlight.

From out of the Shadows...
Stories Filled with Mystery
and Suspense by

MARY DOWNING HAHN

TIME FOR ANDREW
72469-3/$3.99 US/$4.99 Can

DAPHNE'S BOOK
72355-7/$3.99 US/$4.99 Can

THE TIME OF THE WITCH
71116-8/ $3.99 US/ $4.99 Can

STEPPING ON THE CRACKS
71900-2/ $3.99 US/ $4.99 Can

THE DEAD MAN IN INDIAN CREEK
71362-4/ $3.99 US/ $4.99 Can

THE DOLL IN THE GARDEN
70865-5/ $3.50 US/ $4.25 Can

FOLLOWING THE MYSTERY MAN
70677-6/ $3.99 US/ $4.99 Can

TALLAHASSEE HIGGINS
70500-1/ $3.99 US/ $4.99 Can

WAIT TILL HELEN COMES
70442-0/ $3.99 US/ $4.99 Can

THE SPANISH KIDNAPPING DISASTER
71712-3/ $3.99 US/ $4.99 Can

THE JELLYFISH SEASON
71635-6/ $3.50 US/ $4.25 Can

Coming Soon
THE SARA SUMMER
72354-9/ $3.99 US/ $4.99 Can